W9-BBK-374

HIS PREGNANT HOUSEKEEPER

HIS PREGNANT HOUSEKEEPER

BY

CAROLINE ANDERSON

NEW HANOVER COUNTY
PUBLIC LIBRARY
201 CHESTNUT STREET
WILMINGTON, NC 28401

™MILLS & BOON®
Pure reading pleasure™

All the characters in this book have no existence outside the imagination of the author, and have no relation whatsoever to anyone bearing the same name or names. They are not even distantly inspired by any individual known or unknown to the author, and all the incidents are pure invention.

All Rights Reserved including the right of reproduction in whole or in part in any form. This edition is published by arrangement with Harlequin Enterprises II BV/S.à.r.l. The text of this publication or any part thereof may not be reproduced or transmitted in any form or by any means, electronic or mechanical, including photocopying, recording, storage in an information retrieval system, or otherwise, without the written permission of the publisher.

® and TM are trademarks owned and used by the trademark owner and/or its licensee. Trademarks marked with ® are registered with the United Kingdom Patent Office and/or the Office for Harmonisation in the Internal Market and in other countries.

First published in Great Britain 2008
Large Print edition 2008
Harlequin Mills & Boon Limited,
Eton House, 18-24 Paradise Road,
Richmond, Surrey TW9 1SR

© Caroline Anderson 2008

ISBN: 978 0 263 20078 2

Set in Times Roman 16½ on 19 pt.
16-0908-51420

Printed and bound in Great Britain
by Antony Rowe Ltd, Chippenham, Wiltshire

CHAPTER ONE

'WHAT on earth—?'

Daniel paused, thumb poised on his car's remote locking button, and watched the woman in amazement.

She was going to do herself a mischief, struggling about in the dark trying to get that huge mattress into the skip—never mind the fact that it was *his* skip and she had no business putting anything in it, but since she was clearly bent on the task—literally—he had no choice but to intervene.

'Here—let me.'

And shouldering her gently out of the way, he slid his keys into his pocket, seized the mattress and lifted it towards the skip—

'No!'

For someone so tiny, she was surprisingly strong. 'That's the wrong way!' she cried, running round to the other side and hauling on the mattress. 'I'm not putting it *in* the skip, I'm taking it *out*!'

He stopped struggling with it and studied her thoughtfully over the top. It was about shoulder height on her, and he could clearly see her stubborn, defiant chin, tilted slightly up as if daring him to argue. He scanned her face, bare of any make-up, taking in the lank brown hair scraped back into a ponytail, the wide, determined eyes and the firm set of that really very soft, lush mouth. He dragged his eyes from it and met her eyes again. 'Excuse me?'

'I said, I'm taking it out—'

'I heard you. I just don't understand. It's an old mattress. Why would you want to take it out of the skip?'

'Because it's better than the one I've got? For goodness' sake, it's unmarked—or it would have been if someone hadn't put it in the skip. Ridiculous waste. So I'm—recycling it.'

'Re—?' He folded his arms, propping them on

the top of the mattress, and met those fiery eyes over the great divide. Not the physical object that separated them, but the light years that divided their understanding. She *really* wanted this old mattress?

'That's right, and we've only got a minute before the security guard comes back round. Either give me a hand, or get out of my way and let me move it, but don't just stand there leaning on it until he's back!'

Daniel glanced over his shoulder towards the door of the security guard's Portakabin, then back to the girl. 'You want me to help you steal the mattress?' he said incredulously, suppressing the urge to laugh.

'Well, it's hardly stealing, it's been thrown out,' she said logically, and he couldn't argue with that. He'd sanctioned it himself. 'So—what's it to be? Are you getting out of the way so I can do it, or are you going to help me?'

He hesitated a moment too long, because she reached out to grab it and move it herself before he could react.

And he couldn't let her do that. What if she hurt herself? She was only a little bit of a thing. Damn.

'Get out of the way,' he said, sighing in resignation and glancing at the security guard's door again. If he got caught—

He grabbed the handles and lifted. 'Where to?'

'Round the corner—it's really not far.'

It wasn't, but it felt far enough. One end bumped the ground, and he lifted it a bit higher and thought it might be time to take Nick up on his offer of the use of his home gym. His biceps were clearly suffering from lack of exercise—either that or it had been a rather good mattress in its day, which would have surprised him since nothing else coming out of the old hotel was much cop.

But then she stopped, sooner than he was expecting, and fumbled for a key. 'In here,' she said, pushing open a door that led into the derelict rear annexe of the hotel, and leaving him to follow, open-mouthed in surprise, she headed up the stairs. 'Be careful, there aren't any lights—they've cut off the power to this part,' she warned him, then, reaching the top, she opened a door and went into a room.

He paused on the landing to get his breath back, and a smell in the air caught his nose. He sniffed. Damp. Definite, overwhelming damp. No wonder she'd needed a new mattress, he thought, wrestling it through the doorway and wondering if he'd lost his mind.

Yup. Definitely. He shouldn't be doing this, making it easier for her to stay. Nick and Harry would kill him, but—

In the harsh glare of the street light outside, she bent and moved a few things out of the way, then pointed to the space she'd cleared, on a floor scarcely big enough to take the mattress. 'There will do fine,' she said, straightening up, and he got his first proper look at her without the mattress in between them, and it stopped him in his tracks.

She was—pregnant?

Squatting in their hotel, holding up progress on the renovations, screwing up their budget and deadlines, piling on the legal fees, and she was pregnant?

Oh, dear God. It went from bad to worse.

He put the mattress down, just because it was easier than standing there holding it, and she promptly lay down on it, sighed hugely and grinned up at him, her bump sticking up into the air like a little football. Her T-shirt had rucked up to reveal the safety pins holding the bottom of her jeans zip together—or trying to. The baby seemed to have made that impossible, and through the gaps he could see a glimpse of smooth, pale skin, curiously vulnerable in the harsh light.

He had an almost overwhelming urge to reach out his hand and touch it, to trail his fingers over her taut abdomen, to rest his palm against that firm swell and make ludicrous promises—

He dragged his eyes away, to find that she'd tucked her hands behind her head and closed her eyes. She patted the mattress beside her and cracked an eye open, still grinning.

'It's fabulous! So much better than the floor—come on, try it!'

Try it? Lie on it next to her? Was she *mad*? He

listed the reasons in his head why this was such a horrendously bad idea, starting with a) it was stolen—albeit from his own skip!—b) it was out of said skip, and c) she was lying on it, their sitting tenant, their *bête noire*, the thorn in the side of their development, looking sexier than any pregnant woman had a right to look, and she was *asking him to lie down with her*?

He backed hastily towards the door.

'Um—can't. I haven't got time. I need to get home and make a phone call.' To Nick and Harry, to tell them that he'd met their squatter. Their *pregnant* squatter!

Her eyes were unreadable in the confusing light, but her actions weren't. She scrambled to her feet and headed towards him, ducking past on to the landing and going into the next room, a woman on a mission. 'In which case, on your way, do you think you could just get rid of this for me, because it stinks.'

'This what?' he asked, his heart sinking as he followed her.

'This old mattress, of course. What else?'

What else, indeed? He closed his eyes, then opened them and studied her expectant face. Not that he could see much of it in the dark, but he knew what he'd find there if he *could* see. He could hear it in her voice, and he was glad he couldn't see her eyes, or he'd go belly-up like a lovesick poodle, and he really, really wasn't going to do this for her.

He really wasn't—

'You want me to dump a stinking mattress on someone's skip?' he asked, feeling suddenly very tired and confused and wondering what the hell he was doing in here with a pregnant woman who had no business living in their hotel and screwing up their schedule with her nonsense.

She grinned, her teeth flashing white in the gloom, and he felt his heart kick against his ribs. 'Well, it's only swapping it, technically. I'm sure, compared to all the other grief I'm giving them, the developers won't care in the slightest about one miserable smelly mattress. I mean, it wasn't great before, but it got soaked in the rain the other night when the ceiling came down.'

On the mattress? The ceiling had come down

on the mattress of a *pregnant woman*? He swallowed the panic, tried not to think about the public liability implications and followed her further into the room.

She was right. It did stink. More than that—it was ancient, filthy and covered in lumps of ceiling. And she wanted him to carry it down the street in his home town—a town where he was trying to carve out a reputation that would hold him in good stead for the next thirty-odd years—and throw it in his own skip?

Oh, bloody hell, he thought, and grabbed hold of the handles and hefted it. Even sopping wet it weighed considerably less than the other one, such was its quality or the lack of it. He gave it another heave until it was upright, and wet plaster fell to the floor with a crash. 'Open the door,' he said in resignation, and wrestled it down the stairs and out on to the pavement.

'Gosh, it really does stink,' she said, walking along on the other side of it and wrinkling that pretty little nose. 'All that mould—I was worried it was bad for the baby.'

Not nearly as bad as the ceiling would have been, he thought, but he bit his lip and carried the wretched mattress round the corner. Knowing his luck, the security guard would catch them, he thought, and then the game would be up. Fantastic. He could just imagine that conversation!

She halted him at the gateway and peered round it into the car park. 'OK,' she said in a piercing stage whisper, and he stifled a chuckle and dragged the offending article across the car park and heaved it into the skip just as light spilling from the doorway heralded the security guard.

'Hey! What d'you think you're doing?' he yelled, and the girl grabbed his hand and ran for it.

What could he do? She was dragging him, laughter bubbling up in her eyes and bursting out into the night, and her hand was firm and bossy and surprisingly strong.

So he ran with her, catching her as she stumbled at the corner, and pulling her into a darkened doorway a few paces along the road, his hand over her mouth, the firm jut of her pregnancy pressing into him and jiggling as she tried hard not to laugh.

And all he could think about was the softness of her mouth under his hand, the feel of her belly against him, the strength of her hand in his as she'd tugged him away.

Then the baby kicked, a solid little thump against his gut, and the laughter faded, driven out by an urge to protect her so powerful, so immense, that it nearly took his knees out from under him.

He knew nothing about her, other than that she was claiming some title to the hotel and her right to it was being heavily disputed by the son of the late owner, who'd sold it to them just before he'd died. The son himself had assured them that her claim was totally spurious and he'd have her out in no time.

That had sounded fine six weeks ago, but then she'd refused to move, and now Dan had met her, now he'd discovered she was pregnant, that changed everything. Suddenly he needed to find out more about her, to know everything there was to know. His head was telling him it was everything to do with the hotel and nothing to do with her laughing eyes and the feel of that baby's kick against his gut, but his heart knew better.

For the first time in nearly a year, Daniel Hamilton was interested in a woman, and everything else, including his common sense, paled into insignificance.

Her co-conspirator and press-ganged mattress-wrestler stuck his head out of the doorway and scanned the street. 'There's no sign of the security guard. I think he's given up.'

'Good. I didn't think he'd bother much. He's too lazy.' She tipped her head on one side, knowing that she ought to move away but enjoying the feel of his hard, lean body against hers rather too much. 'Well, I suppose I ought to go and find something to eat,' she told him reluctantly, trying to summon some enthusiasm for another tin of cold baked beans, but he just eased away from her, dropping the hands that had settled warmly on her shoulders and leaving her feeling oddly bereft.

'Haven't you eaten?' he said, tipping his head

on one side and studying her with a little frown. She couldn't see his eyes—it was too dark in the doorway—but the look on his face was kind, and he'd heaved mattresses for her. He couldn't be all bad.

'Well—no, I haven't, or I wouldn't be thinking about food,' she explained patiently, and his mouth twitched, as if he was suppressing a laugh.

He stepped out of the doorway into the light of the street lamp, and for the first time she was able to see him clearly. Not the colour of his eyes, but the expression—thoughtful, curious, a little hesitant, maybe? Then he seemed to make up his mind about something, and he straightened up.

'Fancy a take-away?'

'I thought you had to make a phone call?' she said, and could have sworn he went a shade darker.

'It'll keep,' he said gruffly. 'Anyway, I have to eat, too. We can take it down to the beach—my treat.'

The beach sounded OK. She wasn't keen on the idea of going to his house or flat or whatever, but the beach seemed safe enough. Nice, even, and 'my treat' was music to her ears. And she didn't have to be gone long.

'OK,' she said, unwilling to turn down the offer of food, whatever the source. She'd been hungry for weeks—that was pregnancy, of course, because the baby was stealing everything it needed and her diet at the moment was a little hit and miss, to say the least. She wasn't able to earn anything, and every penny she had was destined for legal fees—

'Chinese, Indian, Thai, Italian…?'

'Not Thai,' she said quickly, not yet ready to revisit the emotional minefield that was Thailand. 'Chinese, perhaps?'

'Sure. There's a good one on the front. Come on, we can walk from here—unless you're not feeling up to it?'

She shook her head. 'I'm fine to walk. I'm fit—I'm just hungry and pregnant.'

'Then let's get you some food. Any preferences?'

'King prawns, stir-fried vegetables and egg fried rice,' she said promptly, not holding back if he was offering to buy. He took out his phone, speed-dialled a number and rattled off the order, adding Singapore rice noodles and chicken in ginger and spring onions. Oh, joy, more of her favourites! It was looking even better, she thought, and tried not to drool.

The restaurant was on the sea front, at the bottom of the steep, winding little hill that led down to the beach. She'd eaten there once, with Jamie, when they'd first come back to Yoxburgh. It seemed a lifetime ago.

Two lifetimes—

'Coming in?'

'Sure.'

She got her first proper look at him in the lights of the restaurant as they waited by the take-away counter, and her eyes widened. Her mattress-heaving benefactor was seriously hot! She'd already known he was tall, but now she could see the perfect geometry of his face—the high cheekbones, the chiselled jaw, the firm, full lips—and a body that even in her 'condition' made her pulse crank up a notch.

He was wearing a white shirt with the neck

open and the cuffs turned back, showing strong, lightly tanned forearms and the powerful column of his throat. His shoulders were broad and solid under the shirt, his chest deep, his abdomen flat, his legs long and lean and clad in soft old jeans just snug enough around the hips to hint at things she shouldn't even be considering. Fit, in every sense of the word, and he looked good enough to eat. Or touch, at least. His dark hair was soft and glossy, making her fingers itch to rumple it, and she wondered what her own hair looked like after weeks of washing it in cold water and washing up liquid and letting it air dry.

Dire.

It wasn't speculation, it was fact, and she swallowed hard and dragged her eyes off him. He was so far out of reach it was ridiculous, and she had no idea why he was bothering with her.

Pity, probably, but she wasn't going to walk away from a square meal on the grounds of a moral victory. Not even she was that stupid.

He picked up the bag and led her out of the restaurant and across the road to the prom beside the beach. 'Here?' he asked, pausing by a bench, and she nodded. There was enough light from the street lamps behind to see by, the moon was sparkling on the water, and the food smelt so good she really was starting to drool.

'Perfect,' she said, making herself forget about him and how far out of reach he was and concentrate on the core business. She sat down with one leg hitched up and tucked under the other thigh so she was facing him, and more importantly the food, while he pulled all the containers out of the bag, laid them out on the bench between them and ripped the tops off, then handed her a pair of chopsticks.

'Sorry it's not a fork.'

'Chopsticks are fine,' she said, stripping the paper off them and piling right in, and the first king prawn to hit her teeth made her sigh with joy. 'Oh, boy,' she said round it, and grinned at him. 'Fabulous.'

It was the last thing she said for ages.

'Better?'

She finally seemed to have eaten herself to a

standstill, and her smile was a little embarrassed. 'Oh, yes. I think I'm probably going to burst, but yes, fantastic. Thank you—and thank you for lugging that mattress for me.'

He gave a grunt of laughter. 'Which one?' he asked drily. 'The one you stole, or the one you donated?'

She laughed, and her eyes lit up and sparkled like the sea. 'Both,' she said, then her laughter faded and she turned her head, staring out over the water and catching her full, lush lower lip between her teeth and worrying it gently.

'Penny for them,' he prompted softly after a moment.

She sighed. 'I was just wondering if it was worth it—all the hassle of moving the mattress. I mean, it's not going to be for long, is it? I can't stay there, anyone can see that, but if I don't—well, I won't have any chance of getting anything for my baby, and it's her birthright. She's entitled to it, and I have to stay and fight for her.'

'Her?' he asked, ignoring the rest. There'd be

time to deal with that later, when he'd spoken to Nick and Harry, but for now—

'My baby. She's a girl. They told me when I had the scan. I wanted to know—I mean, it's only the two of us, and I wanted to start getting to know her. That seemed like a good place to start. We can have more meaningful conversations now.'

He didn't even comment on that, just smiled to himself and decided that it was a rather nice idea, if a little wacky. 'Have you got a name for her?'

She laughed. 'Well, it won't be Yoxburgh, that's for sure.'

'Pardon?'

'I'm Iona,' she explained with a smile. 'Named for the place where I was conceived, apparently. It could have been a lot worse. Knowing my mother, I'm lucky it wasn't Glastonbury or Marrakesh!'

He chuckled. 'I have to say Iona's far and away the best of the bunch, but I always did have a weakness for the Scottish islands.' He held out his hand and smiled. 'I'm Daniel,' he said, withholding the rest of his name because he didn't want to spoil this brief interlude. It wouldn't be long before she knew who he was. Time enough to hate him then, he thought, and then stopped thinking for a heartbeat because her hand, slim and firm and a little greasy from the food, gripped his and, like a trip-switch in a power surge, his mind shut down and his body took over.

'So—your daughter, whatever you're going to call her—where will she be born?' he asked, dragging his mind back from oblivion and retrieving his hand, and a shadow crossed Iona's eyes.

'I don't know. It depends.'

'On?'

'Whether I can win my fight.' She sighed. 'It's a long story.'

'I've got time,' he said, shifting so he was facing her and settling back against the bench, his arm propped along the back. He could see her like that, watch her body language, try and get to the root of this problem that was threatening to cause havoc with the development. And he could see her hands, curved protectively over her baby, which wasn't, of course, nearly as important in the great scheme of things as establishing the facts, and yet seemed curiously like the most significant fact at this point.

'It's messy,' she warned, and he nodded.

'I don't doubt it for a moment. It usually is,' he agreed, and waited for her to go on.

She was quiet for a moment longer, then she lifted her head and squared her chin. 'I met Jamie when I was travelling. I'd been dragged round the world from birth—my mother's an anthropologist and a bit of a hippy, and I'd spent my life moving from place to place. I'm not sure she knew who my father was apart from the fact that he was called Rick, but it was irrelevant because he never featured in our lives after I was conceived anyway.

'I'd scraped an education, ricocheting from one international school to another, sometimes taught by my mother when there wasn't a school near enough, which was quite often, and somehow I got enough points in my IB—my International Baccalaureate—to go to university.'

That surprised him, and he sat up a little straighter, intrigued. 'What did you read?'

'Law. I wanted to be a human rights lawyer, but I didn't finish my degree. My mother got some horrible tropical bug midway through my second year and nearly died, and I went to look after her and never went back. She recovered, amazingly, considering how ill she was for a while, but I'd missed too much by then and if I was going back I had to redo the year. I hadn't had a gap year, and I wanted to travel on my own, to follow my own agenda for the first time in my life, so I did, meaning to go back to Maastricht at the start of the next academic year, only of course I didn't. I went to Thailand, and I met Jamie, and we just started travelling together. We backpacked round the world, and I showed him some of the places I'd been to, and then after a year we came back to Yoxburgh to see his father.'

She stopped talking, a frown pleating her brow, and he waited, watching in fascination as emotions chased each other across her face.

'His father, Brian, wasn't well. He wanted

Jamie to stay, to help him run the hotel, but he wouldn't. He wanted to go, and he wanted me to go with him. I refused, so he went anyway and I stayed with Brian, helped him with the hotel and continued my studies part-time. One of the advantages of my upbringing is that I'm multi-lingual, so I've been working as an interpreter part-time and doing translations for a bit of extra cash as well, and I carried on doing that. Brian couldn't afford to pay me, so it was essential, really. Then Jamie came back in November after nearly a year away. I really thought that this time he'd stay, do the decent thing, but I might have known he wouldn't. And if I'd known—well, anyway, yet again he wouldn't stay, not even till Christmas. He blagged some money out of his father and went back to Thailand after a fort-night, caught Japanese encephalitis and died. He never knew about the baby.'

Oh, hell's teeth, Dan thought. This was so much more complicated than they'd imagined. He didn't say he was sorry. It would have been a lie. If he was anything, he was disgusted at the man's careless and irresponsible behaviour, but it wasn't his place to say so and, anyway, there was no real sign of grief on her transparent face, just acceptance. So he kept quiet and watched her, her thumb stroking rhythmically, soothingly over the curve of the baby—a tender, comforting caress for her unborn child.

He couldn't take his eyes off that slowly moving thumb.

After a small, thoughtful pause, she went on quietly, 'Brian was devastated. He had a bad heart, and the shock of Jamie's death was awful. He had a heart attack, and they told him to sell up and settle down, so he put the hotel on the market. He'd managed to get a really good deal from these developers, considering how run-down the place had got, and he was going to make sure the baby was all right. We'd found a house for the three of us to live in, and he was going to give the other half of the money to his other son, Ian. And then, a month before we were due to move, he died, and Ian, who'd never even been to see him until he was on his deathbed, came up to me at the funeral and told me his father had asked him to look after me, so he gave me five hundred pounds and a week to move out.'

He crushed down the anger brought to life by her stark rendition of the facts. 'What about the will?'

'He said he was going to change it,' she told him, and a sad little smile touched her lips. 'Like just about everything else it was on his to-do list, though, and when he died his will was nowhere to be found. He'd told me that in his original will it was all left to Jamie and Ian, and by then Jamie was dead, which was why he wanted to change it, but he obviously never got round to it, and because the will couldn't be found, under the intestacy laws Jamie's share will go to his brother, of course.'

'Isn't the baby entitled to Jamie's half?' Dan suggested, not sure of the facts but thinking of the justice of the situation.

She shrugged. 'Not necessarily. It depends on the wording of the original will, but, since we can't find it, it's all a bit academic. I thought maybe Ian might give the baby something out of goodwill, knowing what his father's wishes had been, but apparently he doesn't have any goodwill where I'm concerned, so my only hope is to prove that the baby is Jamie's and hope that the will turns up and there's a clause in it about issue—you know, children and unborn children and so forth.'

'Is the will likely to turn up?'

'I doubt it. Ian ransacked the place looking for it, because without it probate takes for ever, but he didn't find it and I think the hotel's been cleared now ready for the builders to move in. And Brian was so horrendously untidy and dis-organised that it could have been anywhere. It's probably been thrown out by mistake, but of course I can't go in there and look. I don't have access to the main hotel, only the disused annexe. Anyway, I'm not allowed.'

'Allowed?'

'By the security guard. Site rules. We aren't best friends.'

He made a mental note to organise a search. 'So—what happens now?'

'I stay in the hotel, and I'm a thorn in everyone's side and hold things up in the hope that Ian will give in and help me out for the baby's sake, but I can't have a DNA test done until she's born, and by then I'll have had to move out of the hotel, and that'll be that. And I don't want to move out, because possession is nine-tenths of the law and all that, but I can't have her there. And Ian's refusing to budge without a valid will to force him to give me money. I can't blame him—he doesn't know me from Adam. He'd never met me before the funeral and I haven't seen him since he finished tearing the place apart to look for the will. I've had plenty of threatening letters, though.'

Dan clamped his teeth shut to keep in his thoughts. They were unprintable, and if Ian had wandered into range just then, Dan would cheerfully have hung him out to dry. Lucky for him that he didn't, but Iona's situation was infinitely more complicated than they'd imagined, and the implications of her sorry little account of the events leading up to this point were huge. He needed to speak to Nick and Harry, but it was too late now, and anyway, Iona was yawning her head off and he needed to walk her home.

Home?

He nearly snorted in disbelief that she was living like that, her few possessions scattered around her on the tired carpet, the ceiling down in the next room, the all-pervading stench of mould filling the building. There was a lingering aura of it hanging over them even now, in the sea air—because of handling the mattress, or because her clothes were permeated by it? Whatever, it couldn't be healthy living in that atmosphere.

There was no power in the annexe, no light, although the water was still on. That, apparently, was a legal requirement, and they were still at the point of trying to negotiate her removal with the solicitors.

Or they had been.

What they did now in the light of this new information he had no idea.

'You're tired. Let me walk you back,' he said,

and she started scraping all the leftovers into one container, squashed them down and put a lid on.

'For tomorrow,' she said, her words tinged with defiance as if she was daring him to challenge her. 'Unless you want it?'

He lifted his hands. 'Be my guest,' he said, and vowed to sort her situation out once and for all. First thing in the morning, he was contacting the others, and if he had anything to say about it, she'd only spend this one night on her recycled mattress in that dank and dismal room with her leftover Chinese for company.

She wasn't going to let him in, but he insisted on checking that it was safe, that nobody had broken in. Then he went out and listened to her as she closed the door and locked it. There was the scrape of keys and slide of bolts, and he wondered who she was trying to keep out. He stood there, deep in thought, worrying about her, before finally walking round the corner to his car in the car park. The security guard came out of his Portakabin and hailed him as he unlocked his car and the lights flashed.

'You off, Guv?'

'Yup. Everything all right?'

'Fine. Someone put a mattress on the skip, but I chased them off,' he said. 'They were only kids.'

Daniel kept a straight face with difficulty.

'Happens all the time,' he said and, lifting a hand in farewell, he got into his car and drove home.

Home to his newly built, just commissioned house, with its five bedrooms and guest wing, stunning views of the sea and only one person rattling around in it.

Guilt pricked at him as he walked through the door and turned on the lights. Guilt, and shame. Not because of the opulence, because it wasn't opulent at all. If anything, it was stark and spare, with nothing to detract from the purity of the spaces. The house flowed naturally from one area to another—uncluttered, simple, a perfect symphony of glass and brick and wood and stone working in harmony.

And empty.

Hence the guilt, because all this space, for one person—that was the obscenity. That, and the fact that Iona, alone and without support, was fighting a battle she should never have had to fight, in the squalid environment of that near-derelict hotel annexe. Fighting it not really with them, but with her baby's uncle, and not for herself but for the child.

He'd have to talk to Nick and Harry first thing in the morning and see what they could sort out, because she couldn't stay there, even without the pressing consideration of their refurbishment schedule and the fact that that wing of the hotel was due for demolition in the next couple of weeks.

They'd have to make sure she was all right, find her somewhere safe to go, he thought. He'd get on to it first thing in the morning. At least it didn't look like rain tonight.

His conscience as clear as he could get it, he went up to bed and lay staring out over the moonlit sea and wondered if she was asleep yet on her new mattress, and if she was more comfortable, and if she was safe behind all the locks and bolts, in that dismal room with her scant possessions and her leftover Chinese meal in its little box.

When the rain lashing on the window woke him in the small hours, he lay there listening to it and wondering if the ceiling in the new room was safe or if that, too, was going to fall down on her while she slept.

Two hours later, unable to sleep again and calling himself every kind of a fool, he went down to the kitchen, made a savagely strong espresso and sat sipping it with the doors flung wide while the sky lightened and the pale disc of a watery sun rose out of the sea and sparkled on the water, tranquil and soothing, and wondered what they could do to help her.

CHAPTER TWO

'WE NEED a meeting.'

Nick groaned, and Dan heard the rustle of bed-clothes and a sleepy murmur from Georgie in the background.

'Do you have any idea what the time is?' Nick growled.

'Five-thirty?'

'And you think that's *reasonable? On Sunday morning*?'

'I've met our squatter.'

There was a heartbeat of silence. 'And?'

'She's pregnant.'

Another silence. Then something unprintable, and the sound of bedclothes and then footsteps. 'We need a meeting.'

Dan chuckled. 'That was my line. Where? And when?'

'Yours—since you're up, you can cook us breakfast. Give me half an hour. And I'll let you ring Harry. If he's got any sense, he'll tell you to go to hell.'

He didn't. He was actually rather ruder, but since his suggestion was anatomically impossible, Dan chuckled and hung up, then had a quick shower and filled the oven with frozen pastries while he made the coffee, then pressed the button to open the gates.

'This had better be good,' Harry muttered, wandering in moments later in shorts and a T-shirt that he could well have slept in, his jaw dark with stubble and his hair rumpled and Nick hard on his heels.

'Oh, it's good. Hi, Nick. Sorry about this. Coffee?'

'Too right. Can I smell croissants?'

'Yup. Sit down, I'll bring them over.'

He poured three mugs of coffee—slightly weaker this time, since his stomach was still rebelling after the last one—and brought the whole lot to the low coffee table in the middle of the seating area and put it down.

'So—this pregnant squatter,' Harry said round a mouthful of almond pastry and gooey marzipan. 'Is she going to be a problem?'

'Could be.' He picked up a *pain au chocolat* and sat back, studying it intently. 'Apparently the baby is Brian Dawes's other son's child.'

Nick choked on his croissant and dumped his coffee mug back on to the table. *'What?'*

'I said—'

'I heard what you said. I didn't even know there was another son. What are the implications?'

'And how the hell can we throw her out if she's pregnant?' Harry put in, his almond croissant forgotten.

'I don't think we can—and there isn't another son, not any more. He's dead. But she can't stay there, so I have a plan.'

They groaned and exchanged glances, then looked back at him, scepticism writ large on their faces.

'Which is?' Nick prompted.

'We need to get her out of the hotel. Move her somewhere appropriate—somewhere where the ceiling isn't going to fall in on her if it rains.'

Harry narrowed his eyes, then his jaw sagged. 'The ceiling fell in?'

'On the mattress. That's how I met her—she was nicking a mattress out of the skip at the hotel to replace it.'

'And you stopped her, and she told you all this?' Nick said, and he ran his hand round the back of his neck and pressed his lips together.

'Not exactly.'

'So—what, exactly?'

So he told them about the mattress-swapping, and once they'd finished howling with laughter and ribbing him about being a sucker, he asked them what they would have done.

They shrugged thoughtfully, and he nodded.

'I rest my case. Anyway, I took her down to the sea front and we had a take-away, and I found out tons about her, and about this situation, and it really isn't cut and dried. If the baby is the dead son's, and she's assured me it is, then I think she—the baby—might be entitled to his part of the estate.'

'You know that?'

'I don't know. I think so. I've been on the net. It's confusing. "Unborn" seems to have several connotations—like already conceived and not yet born, and to be conceived and born at some point in the future, but there's an expression—*en ventre sa mère*. In the womb of the mother. It's not really clear, and without a look at the will it's not possible to know if she would inherit, but there's a slight problem—apparently the will's disappeared. We need to get her legal advice.'

'We do?'

'Yes, we do,' he said shortly. 'We can't mess this up. I can just see the headlines now—PREGNANT WOMAN KILLED BY FALLING ROOF— NEW OWNERS DENY RESPONSIBILITY.'

'I'm surprised you didn't drag our legal team out of bed at five-thirty on a Sunday morning to ask them to join us,' Nick said mildly, with just a touch of rancour.

Dan rubbed a hand through his hair, embarrassed to admit that if he'd had a home number he might have been tempted. 'We need to take advice on this, guys—it's important. And we need to get her out.'

'I agree,' Harry said, frowning. 'We do—need legal advice, before we move her out and end up responsible for her welfare and incurring huge legal bills for a fight which isn't ours. In fact, none of this is our concern. We should just get her moved out and let Social Services take care of her.'

Dan frowned at Harry. 'Like you'd do that. Harry, she's probably seven months pregnant.'

'Exactly. And there are people professionally employed to deal with situations like that. It's not as if the baby's anything to do with any of us.'

'That didn't stop you before.'

Harry's eyes flicked away momentarily. 'That was different.'

'Was it? And I'm only talking about getting her legal advice, not marrying her—'

'Time out, boys,' Nick interrupted, sitting

forward, all business now. 'Dan's right, we need to take legal advice, and we need to get her safely out of there before any harm comes to her. Her presence in the building is irrelevant to her claim, anyway, since we've bought it.'

'Except that she doesn't have a tenancy agreement so we can't legally kick her out,' Dan reminded him. 'And if any more of that ceiling comes down before Monday and injures her, I don't know where we stand.'

'So what the hell do we do?'

'I have an idea.'

'Why doesn't that fill me with confidence?' Harry said darkly, and Dan laughed.

'I can't imagine.'

'Going to share?' Nick suggested.

He shook his head. 'Not till I've thought it through and discussed it with her.'

Harry frowned. 'Don't you think you should discuss it with us first? As your business partners and co-owners of the development?'

'No,' he said bluntly. 'I don't. If there's anything to tell you, I'll report back.'

'You do that. There's a substantial chunk of my royalties riding on this venture,' Harry reminded him.

'You've got till nine on Monday, then I'm phoning the law team,' Nick said briskly, and got to his feet. 'Now, I'm going home, and if I'm really lucky, the kids'll still be asleep and I can go back to bed with my wife.'

He walked out, leaving Harry there watching Dan in a thoughtful silence.

'What?'

'I should be asking you that,' Harry said.

'Don't bother. It's only an idea. It probably won't come to anything.'

Harry stood up slowly and let his breath out on a sigh. 'A word of advice,' he said. 'Don't get sucked in, Dan. It's all too easy.'

'You can talk.'

'Absolutely. I think I'm precisely the person to talk—and I can see you falling into exactly the same trap.'

'Hardly.'

He put a hand on Dan's shoulder. 'Just be

careful, eh?' he murmured, and then left him alone to work out the finer details of his plan.

She turned him down.

He hadn't expected it at all, but he probably should have done. When he'd thought it was late enough—bearing in mind her interest in this problem was rather different from theirs—he'd gone round and knocked on the door to the annexe.

He heard her yell something, heard the sound of her running lightly down the stairs, then, on the other side of the door, she stopped.

'Who is it?' she said.

'Dan.'

'Dan?' she said, her voice surprised. 'Daniel? As in last night?'

'Yup—Iona, can I come in?'

There was a rattle and a clatter, the sound of locks turning, and then finally she opened the door, her eyes wary. 'What can I do for you?'

'I've got a proposition for you,' he began, and she started to shut the door. He jammed his foot in it.

'Not that sort of proposition,' he said, feeling

inexplicably weary. Although perhaps not inexplicably, since this woman and thoughts of her
had kept him awake for the better part of the
night. He pushed the door gently open and went
in, shutting it behind him. 'You're quite safe with
me, Iona,' he said without moving any further. 'I
just want to talk to you. May I come in?'

'I thought you had,' she huffed, then sniffed the
air and stared at the brown paper carrier in his
hand. 'What's that?'

'Breakfast—coffee and croissants.'

She all but snatched the bag from him, shoving
her nose into it and inhaling the smell that drifted
up from the coffee. She moaned softly and threw
him a megawatt smile. 'Come in and mind where
you walk,' she said, beaming, and led the way up
the stairs past a fresh mess of plaster and wall-
paper that had obviously fallen down in the night.
Tons of it, leaving a gaping hole in the roof.

Jeez. How much worse could it get?

Her room, he was glad to see, seemed dry
still. She sat down cross-legged on the conten-
tious mattress with her back against the wall

and the bag in front of her, fished out the coffee cups he'd picked up at the café down the road and handed him one, then, ripping open the bag of pastries, she waded in without another word.

Lord, she must have been starving, he thought, frowning. She looked up and stopped chewing, then rubbed her mouth on the back of her hand and straightened up, gesturing to the bag. 'Sorry. Never did have any manners when I was hungry. Would you—?'

He shook his head. 'I've had some.' Hours ago, when he'd dragged his friends out of bed to share the glad tidings. 'Why don't I talk while you eat?' he suggested, settling himself on the edge of the mattress, against the wall, at right angles to her so he could see her, and after a second she nodded and carried on, pausing only to rip the top off the coffee and sip it with a groan of ecstasy that made his blood run hot.

'Well, go on, then,' she prompted when she was halfway through the second croissant and he still hadn't said anything.

'Um—I wanted to offer you a job,' he said. 'As my housekeeper.'

She coughed, swallowed and stared at him. 'Housekeeper? Me?'

He shrugged. 'You need somewhere to live, I need someone to live in and look after my house and cook me supper in the evenings and keep the chaos under control—and if you were able to keep this hotel running, I'm sure my house would be a walk in the park.'

'I can't,' she said flatly after a nail-biting pause. 'I can't move out. If the developers knew I was out, they'd demolish this bit and I'll lose my home. I hardly even dare leave to get food in case they change the locks. And as soon as I'm out, I cease to be a problem to them and if I'm not a problem, then I haven't got a prayer of getting them on my side to help me fight Ian.'

He contemplated telling her that he *was* one of the developers and he was definitely on her side, but thought better of it. Just for now.

'What if I offer to help you fight the case?'

'Why the hell should you do that? I mean, I

know I shouln't look a gift horse and all that, but I've been round the world a few times, never mind the block. I've met people you wouldn't believe, seen things that would make your hair curl. I know all about human nature, Daniel, and, trust me, it's nasty. So forgive me if I'm not in a hurry to fall into your arms and let you carry me out of here on your white charger—'

'I was offering you a job,' he pointed out mildly, wondering what it would feel like if she fell into his arms and let him carry her off, in his BMW if not on a charger, and decided that fantasising would get him precisely nowhere.

'Yeah, right. No strings and all that.'

'Well, no. There are strings. I expect you to keep the house clean and tidy, to cook me something rather healthier than the average take-away, which is what I exist on at the moment, and to do my laundry. And I'll pay you, and you'll have a home for you and your daughter where the ceiling won't fall in and the lights come on when you press a switch and you won't go to bed hungry and wake up with no prospect of food—'

He broke off, because her eyes had filled with tears and the sight was threatening to unravel him. She blinked hard and looked away.

'Um—why?' she asked.

Good question. He had no intention of giving her the right answer. Either of them. She didn't need to know he was involved in the project, and she *certainly* didn't need to know that she'd haunted his sleep and wasn't doing much for his waking hours, either!

'Supply and demand,' he said instead, sticking to the job angle. 'Why don't you look at the house before you give me an answer?'

'I'll want references,' she said, eyeing him as if she still wasn't quite sure he was for real, and he laughed.

'I don't doubt it. I could return the favour.'

Her smile was sad and a little crooked. 'Brian's dead. He would have told you what you wanted to know. There isn't anyone else, but I don't lie and I don't cheat and I work hard. How about a trial period? Say—a month? That should give us both time to see if we can live together.'

'You haven't even seen the house,' he said, but she just laughed.

'You said it has electricity and the roof doesn't leak. What more do I need to know?'

'Oh, my God.'

She saw him glance across at her, but she didn't take her eyes off the big iron gates as they glided open at the touch of a button and the car eased past them down a drive between high, clipped hedges. The right hand hedge carried on straight down the boundary, but the left hand one turned sharply and the drive widened out in front of a house.

At least, she assumed it was a house, but it was a house unlike any she'd ever set foot in, and light years from the door-in-the-middle-and-windows-either-side house of convention.

A great white stucco block, much wider than it was high, with a flat roof that projected out into a deep overhang, it had a big, plain black door to the left of centre, three small black-framed windows scattered apparently randomly across the blank white expanse of the elevation facing her, and a single tall window on the left of the front door stretching up almost to the roof. There was a long, low garage block set at the far end at right angles, connected to the main house by a single-storey section that, apart from a lonely door, was featureless.

It should have been ugly, she thought, but it wasn't; although it certainly wasn't pretty, there was a kind of stark simplicity, a rightness about it all that was curiously calming.

Not that it was calming her at the moment. Not a chance, because she just knew that when that door opened, the house was going to blow her socks off, and she could hardly wait.

He pulled up in front of the garage beside a skip half-full of building materials and rubbish, and she realised it was either newly built or in the final stages of a major renovation. She couldn't tell from there, but no doubt once the door was opened all would be revealed.

She glanced across at Daniel. He still hadn't said a word, but he got out of the car and came round and opened her door and helped her out on to the tarmacked drive and, with anticipation fizzing in her veins, she followed him. He slipped a key in the lock, turned it and pushed the door open, and gestured for her to go in.

She took two steps, slowed to a halt and stared in awe. The far wall was glass. All glass, from floor to ceiling, side to side—all of it, a wall of glass, and beyond it, beyond the smooth stone terrace and the manicured emerald lawn that stretched away like a giant billiard table towards the horizon, was the sea.

She took another step forward. She didn't even notice the house. It was irrelevant. The sea was calling her. The sun was sparkling off its ruffled waters today but she could picture it with an oily, flat calm, or a lazy swell, or crashing against the unseen shore in the teeth of a gale—knew it would reflect every mood of nature, every breath of wind and drop of rain changing it, recharging her batteries, renewing her spirit, filling her soul. It was stunning, amazing and awe-inspiring, and she felt the threatening prickle of tears.

She loved the sea. Needed it. It was in her

blood—something to do with Iona, with the island where she had begun? And he had this all the time, every time he glanced up or opened his eyes. Amazing. Lucky, lucky man.

She dragged her eyes from it and looked around, and then, finally, the house itself registered, and she felt her jaw sag.

They were in a staircase hall that ran from front to back, empty except for the cantilevered timber treads of the stairs that seemed to grow from the wall beside her on her left, and a huge canvas propped against the opposite wall—an evocative, swirling abstract that captured the essence of the sea.

She walked past them towards the glass, looking around her now, taking it all in—the smooth white walls soaring up towards the roof, the slate-flagged floor, almost black and honed to a fine, soft finish, which carried on out to the terrace beyond. There was an opening on the right before the glass wall—not a doorway, just a wide gap leading her on—and as she looked through it, she saw a huge open-plan living room with big squashy sofas grouped around a low table set in the middle of a beautiful bold woollen rug. The room was partly divided, so that the kitchen area was tucked round a corner out of sight, and yet arranged so that as you were working in it, you could see the sea. And it was beautiful.

Stunning. So simple, the lines so clean, again like the frontage almost monastic, and—oh, there must be a word, just a single word for it if only she could—

Pure.

That was it. It was *pure.* It gave her a feeling of tranquillity and calm that washed away all the stress of the past few months, as if all that were somehow irrelevant. How amazing, that a house could do that as soon as you stepped inside.

She turned and looked at Daniel, met his eyes—wary, watchful, waiting for her reaction.

'It's beautiful,' she said softly, and to her surprise she saw the tension go out of him, as if her insignificant opinion actually made a difference to him, which was absurd. 'Stunning. I thought it would be from the front. It's like one of those fabulous iconic Modernist houses from the thirties that I've seen in books—don't ask me who by, I'm hopeless with names, but—oh, wow, Daniel! It's just amazing. All that space, light—can you feel it, or is it just me?' she added, suddenly unsure and wondering if he'd laugh at her for going over the top.

He did—a soft huff of laughter. 'I think you could be over-egging the pudding a bit. Not that I'm not flattered, but they were in a different league. But I'm glad you like it.'

She shook her head, sure at least about that. 'Oh, I love it. It's amazing, and it's not in a different league at all. Well, I don't think so, not that I know anything at all really, but I think you're doing the architect a disservice. It's fabulous. I wonder who designed it? I'd love to meet him. Is it new, or did you refurbish it?'

'No, it's new.'

He suddenly looked a little awkward, and then something occurred to her, and she sucked in her breath and tilted her head a fraction. 'Oh, my God,' she said softly, almost under her breath. 'It was you, wasn't it? You designed it! Designed it and built it for yourself.'

The tension was back, and she knew she was right. 'You did, didn't you?' she said, more positively now. 'You were the architect!'

He nodded, his mouth kicking up on one side in a tentative smile. 'I was really lucky to get the plot. There had been a house here, a much simpler and smaller house but in a similar style, but the lady who lived in it couldn't afford to maintain it, and it fell into disrepair. In the end there was a fire and it had to be demolished, and the planners insisted that the new house was in keeping with the original, which suited me down to the ground. I've always loved Modernist architecture, and I've been dreaming about building a house like this for years, but I never thought I'd get the chance. Well, not till I was a lot older, anyway, but I was in the right place at the right time—and I had luck on my side.'

Luck? Try money, she thought, and then another thought came, and she felt the hairs stand up on the back of her neck. 'Oh, good grief. You're seriously rich, aren't you?' she said, staring at him as if his appearance would give her any clues. None as glaringly obvious as the house, but his car and clothes reeked of quality. She groaned. How could she have been so stupid? 'You're probably a millionaire—and several times over.'

He gave a self-deprecating laugh. 'Not several. I've got pretty stonking debts at the moment, but I got lucky in New York—picked up some real estate with potential, took a few gambles that paid off, built on what seemed like a successful formula. I sold up and pulled out recently— nearly a year ago.' A muscle tensed in his jaw, and she wondered why.

She didn't ask, restraining her usually unrestrained tongue for a change. Instead she concentrated on the successful formula bit. 'So—how long did it take you to build this property empire?' she said, scanning his face for any further clues, but there were none.

He shrugged. 'Ten years, I suppose. I bought

my first flat when I was twenty-one—that was the start of it. But it was only in New York four years ago that things really started to take off. And because of my connections in the property world I've had opportunities others wouldn't have had.'

And a gift, she realised, despite his modesty. An extraordinary talent. And she hadn't even seen the house yet, not really.

She swung back and looked around again, taking in the detail she'd missed the first time. It was simply furnished. It would have to be, of course, to work, and it did work. It worked in spades, and yet it looked welcoming. The dining table, like the coffee table and the stair treads, was sleek, solid oak, carefully placed between the kitchen and the glass wall and beside the seating area, so that wherever you were in the room you would be able to see the sea and be part of all that was going on.

And something had been going on. There were crumbs and mugs and plates scattered all over the coffee table, and on the worktop in the kitchen was an empty plastic milk bottle.

'Sorry about the mess,' he said, but she just shook her head.

'At least I can believe you now when you say you need someone to look after it.'

He snorted softly, and she smiled to herself and walked over to the kitchen, running her fingers reverently over the slate worktop— honed, like the floor, not polished, because that would reflect too much light and be hard to work on, but a soft, silken-smooth matt finish, almost black, contrasting sharply with the flat, high-gloss cabinet doors. They were white, stark like the house and yet curiously understated, and the hob was a featureless sheet of black glass let into the stone of the worktop.

'Think you could work in this kitchen?' he asked, and she laughed softly.

'No. I'd stand here all day staring out over the sea and dreaming,' she said honestly.

'You get used to it after a while.'

She shook her head. 'Never. It's stunning, Daniel. I'd love to see the rest—will you show me?'

His smile was just a flicker, but his eyes—

hazel, she realised belatedly, with flecks of gold—were warm. 'Of course,' he said, and led her back to the entrance hall.

She pointed at another opening off the far side, this time with a sliding partition pulled half across it. 'So—what's through there?'

He pulled the partition closed before she could stick her head in and look. 'My studio. It's a mess. You don't need to worry about that.'

He took her upstairs and showed her the bedrooms, each one facing the sea with that same wall of glass. Even the bathroom in the master suite had full-length glass, so you could lie in the tub and stare out over that wonderful, endless sea.

'Oh, wow!' she said under her breath.

And then found herself picturing him lying there in the water, a glass of wine in one hand, a book in the other and the sea stretched out in front of him, and her eyes were drawn to him.

What would he look like—?

No! She mustn't think like that! Not if she was going to have to live with him, be his housekeeper.

Housekeeper, for heaven's sake!

What a crazy word. It conjured up an image of some middle-aged, dumpy mother figure in a grey serge dress and starched, blindingly white apron, bustling around and keeping the servants in order.

Not an otherwise homeless, pregnant woman of twenty-four with an unfinished degree and no real idea of where she went from here.

She felt her smile fade, and pasted it back in place.

'Very impressive,' she said, scanning the wet-room area of the bathroom and wondering how easy those stone tiles would be to clean. That's it, stick to the practicalities, she reminded herself, and followed him back into the master bedroom, keeping her eyes firmly away from the big, rumpled and deeply inviting bed set opposite the windows.

'No curtains,' she said, suddenly noticing that. 'There aren't any anywhere. Is that because you've only just moved in? I noticed the skip on the drive and a pile of building stuff.'

'I have just moved in, but there aren't any curtains because I don't need them.'

And he pressed a button on the wall and the view disappeared, leaving them in a softer light. He pressed it again, and it went darker, then lighter until the glass was clear once more and the sea reappeared.

'Smart windows,' he said.

She was amazed. 'How do they work?'

'They pass a current across the crystal and it realigns it, cutting out the light.'

She frowned at him, not at all sure she understood. 'So you won't have curtains for insulation? Is that entirely environmentally sound?'

His mouth quirked into a smile. 'Not entirely. If I was being entirely environmentally sound, I wouldn't have a wall of glass, but I've done everything else I can. They're triple glazed with Low-E glass, and by cutting out the light transmission they save energy and keep the heat in in the winter and out in the summer. And they only use a very small amount of energy to change the opacity, then the current goes off. They're as good as they can be.'

'Guilty conscience in the face of all this conspicuous consumerism, Daniel?' she murmured, and had the pleasure of watching him frown slightly.

'Not at all. The whole house is heavily insulated, the roof's tiled with solar panels, the heating's run from a ground-source heat pump powered by solar cells, it's got grey-water and rain-water recovery for flushing the loos and watering the garden, there's a heat recovery system for the ventilation in the winter and because of the design of the windows and the roof it stays cool and doesn't need air-conditioning in the summer—I think I'm allowed the odd toy on top of those impeccable credentials. And it's not really conspicuous consumerism. It's a showcase for my work, and it's what the modern consumer is looking for.'

He looked a little defensive, as if he didn't expect her to believe him. She stared at him, then turned away so he didn't see the smile tugging at her mouth. So he was a closet eco-warrior as well as an architect, was he, juggling commercial pressure and ethics? And a champion mattress-wrestler and provider of breakfast, to boot.

Not to mention thrower of lifelines on the job and accommodation front. And what a lifeline!

She went back on to the landing, past the head of the stairs, and glanced into the other rooms. They were unfurnished, confirming her earlier suspicion that he'd only just moved in, and one of them was stacked with boxes. Boxes he'd been rummaging in.

She looked beyond the mess and saw a doorway to what was probably a bathroom. Another one? 'Are all the bedrooms *en suite*?' she asked a little incredulously.

He lounged against the doorframe and grinned. 'Will you shoot me down in flames if I say it seemed reasonable?' he said, making her wonder about the definition of reasonable. Just now she'd settle for a bowl of hot water instead of cold to wash in!

'As if,' she said, and smiled back. 'So—which one would be mine?'

'Oh, none of these,' he said, sounding slightly shocked. 'Yours is downstairs.'

And he led her down the stairs and along a

hallway while she kicked herself for imagining that staff would even conceivably have a room with a sea view, but then he opened a door into another hall that led in turn to a small sitting room. Well, small by his standards, no doubt. Not by hers. There was a bedroom off it, with a brand-new bed still in its wrapper facing the to-die-for view, a comparatively modest but still very generous bathroom, and a little kitchen area with a small table and chairs set to one side.

They must be in the single-storey area beside the garage, she realised—a whole suite of rooms, like a little self-contained flat, with its own entrance from the drive and yet another bedroom behind the first, the only habitable room in the house apart from her kitchen that didn't face the sea.

And this would be hers? This whole area?

As if he could read her mind, he spoke softly behind her. 'I thought if you and the baby had this bit, you'd have everything you need. The kitchen's pretty simple, but you won't need it if you're cooking for me anyway, except to do the odd thing on your days off. I imagine you'll eat with me?'

Would she?

Only if she could cook well enough that he wouldn't throw the food at her!

She felt a sudden moment of blinding panic. What if she failed? What if she couldn't do this? What if he hated living with her? She wasn't worried about her reaction to him; she could live with anyone, she'd had a lifetime of doing it. But he might find her baby noisy, or her very presence in his house disturbing. Or her habit of speaking her mind without engaging her brain first. She really ought to stop doing that.

His studio was just next to her, she realised, although the doors were miles apart. What if the baby cried and disturbed him while he was working? Maybe he didn't do much work there—perhaps it was just a home office and most of the time he was somewhere else? She wished she'd had a chance to see it. Maybe it would have told her more about him.

Like whether he could live with her?

'So—what do you think?' he asked, and she

thought she could detect tension in his voice again. 'Will it do?'

'Do?'

'You know—for you and the baby. It was designed to be flexible, a guest suite for longer stay visitors, an annexe for dependent relatives, a staff flat, but it wasn't really designed with a baby in mind. I suppose I could carpet it—that might make it more baby-friendly. What do you think?'

'Of the house? Or the carpet?'

'Either. Both. All of it.'

She contemplated teasing him, but relented. Apart from the fact that she not only needed but *wanted* this job more than she would have believed possible, she couldn't lie to him. Not when her insignificant opinion seemed so important to him.

'I think it's the most beautiful house I've ever seen,' she said softly. 'And I'm sorry I teased you about the conspicuous consumerism.'

His mouth twitched and his eyes creased in a smile. 'You do have a valid point, to an extent, even if I try and justify it on work grounds.' He hesitated. 'So—could you live here? *Would* you? Will you take the job?'

She buried her doubts about her abilities and let her smile bloom. 'Oh, absolutely. I don't know how well I can do it, but I'll do my best and I'm sure I can learn. If you'll give me a chance to prove myself, I can't imagine anywhere I'd rather be. It's stunning. And for what it's worth, I think you've created something far more than just a house here, something utterly exceptional, and I think it's breathtaking.'

Breathtaking?

He smiled to himself, a little wryly. Odd, how much her opinion mattered to him, but it did, and her enthusiasm for it was absurdly uplifting.

'Thank you,' he said, genuinely humbled by her praise. And then he thought about the rest— the job he'd created out of nowhere, the fact that she was moving out of the hotel against her better judgement without being in full possession of the facts about him and his vested interest, and he felt a flicker of guilt for not telling her that he was involved with the project.

Time for that later.

She'd probably be mad with him for not telling her, but by then she'd be out and safe, she'd be getting the best legal advice that money could buy and her future would be on the way to being more secure.

His conscience could live with that.

CHAPTER THREE

IONA demanded references, of course.

'You can't say you weren't warned. Just because you're a fantastic architect doesn't mean you aren't an axe-murderer,' she pointed out not unreasonably.

Dan tucked the 'fantastic' thing in his pocket to massage his ego with later, and let the axe-murderer go. 'So who would you find acceptable as a referee? Bearing in mind that it's Sunday.'

She shrugged. 'Someone who's known you for years? A doctor? Teacher? Vicar?' She eyed him doubtfully. 'Probably not a vicar,' she amended, and he felt perversely insulted.

'How about Harry Kavenagh?'

She frowned. 'The guy on the telly? The foreign correspondent or some such?'

'That's the one.'

'You know him?' she said, disbelief in her tone.

He nodded. 'We've been friends for years, and we're business partners now. He's married to my sister. They live round the corner.'

She shook her head. 'Uh-uh. That's too close a relationship. Try again.'

'Nick Barron—heard of him? He's a mover and shaker in the City—nice guy. He's another business partner.'

'No. He probably has his own hitman,' she said, and he thought of Nick throwing away his bachelor lifestyle to bring up his sister's children, and laughed at the absurdity of her suggestion.

'I don't think so. How about Nick's wife? She's another architect, but she's up to her eyes in nappies at the moment. She's known me since primary school—will she do? I doubt if she's got a hit man. Or is that too close, as well?'

'How close is close?'

He grinned wryly and went for honesty. 'I

kissed her once when we were kids. She slapped me. I wasn't tempted to try again.'

Her mouth twitched. 'She'll do. Not ideal, but she'd tell me if she thought you were dodgy. A woman wouldn't lie.'

He snorted softly. That didn't tally with his experience, but he didn't want to go into the sordid details of Kate's litany of lies and deception, so he let it pass. 'I'll call her,' he said, and when she answered, he said economically, 'Hi, Georgie. I need a character reference—for a potential employee. In the absence of a vicar, you're top of her list. Care to oblige?'

'Oh, Dan! What's it worth?' she teased, and he gave a little huff of laughter.

'She's here with me now—her name's Iona. I'll put you on hands-free,' he said, pressing the button that would ensure he got both sides of this conversation, and crossing his fingers in his pocket that Nick hadn't mentioned Iona's name. Don't blow it, Georgie, he prayed, and set the phone down. 'Georgie? Have you got me?'

'I've got you,' she said, her voice clearly audible in the room. 'Hi, there.'

He looked at Iona and tipped his head towards the phone, and she straightened up.

'Um—hi, Georgie. I gather you've known Daniel for a while?'

'Try twenty-five years,' Georgie said with a dry chuckle. 'Man and very irritating boy.'

'Can I trust him?'

'*Trust* him?' Georgie said, her voice slightly shocked. 'With what? Your safety? Your reputation? Your virtue?'

To his surprise, Iona laughed. 'It's a little late for my reputation, and my virtue's long gone. I was thinking of my safety.'

'Absolutely. Well, all of them, really. Put it like this, we trust him with our children, and he's fabulous with them. They adore him, but then they would. He's a sweetheart—a genuinely nice guy. Nothing's too much trouble.'

He rolled his eyes at that. Iona, catching it, shot him a searching look, and smiled. 'Yes. I think you're right. And he has a very nice house.'

'He's shown you the house?' Georgie said, clearly surprised.

Iona, oblivious to his frantic attempts at telepathy, said blithely, 'Oh, yes—well, it was sort of relevant. He wants me to be his house-keeper.'

'*Housekeeper?*' Georgie squealed, and his heart sank. 'Good grief, I thought he wanted a PA or something, Iona!' and he heard a muffled exclamation in the background.

'Is there a problem with that?' Iona asked cautiously.

'Shush, Nick, she wanted to talk to me, not you, you can talk to Dan in a minute. Um—no, no problem, I just didn't know he was looking for a housekeeper, but I can understand it. He's pathologically untidy. Although he's been a neat-freak since he got that house—'

'And I can't cook,' Dan said firmly, picking up the phone and switching off the hands-free before Nick said something to land him in the doo-doo. 'And I'm lousy at ironing. Anyway, the novelty's wearing off.'

'I didn't think it would last. Iona, don't listen to him; you really don't want to work for him in the house, he's a nightmare—'

'She can't hear you now—'

'Tell me she's not our squatter,' Nick said, cutting Georgie off and chipping in.

'What?' Georgie was shrieking.

'Thanks for the reference,' he said blithely, and cut them off fast before either one of them said something to put Iona off.

Iona, however, oblivious to the furore no doubt breaking out at Nick and Georgie's house, was studying him like an insect. 'Pathologically untidy? I would have said neat-freak, but then there's the mess in here, and the boxes upstairs, and you hadn't made your bed,' she said thoughtfully. 'And considering the house is virtually empty because you've only just moved in, there's not a lot to make a mess with. So maybe she was right the first time. Or will the neat-freak in you win?'

He gave a grunt of laughter. 'It rather depends on the day of the week, and you haven't seen my studio. The neat-freak's not winning in there, I can assure you.'

She studied him in silence for another second, then smiled back. 'Fine. She sounds nice. Decent. I'll take it.'

'The job?'

She nodded, and he let out the breath he'd been holding and smiled. 'Great. When do you want to start?'

She laughed. 'How about some time in the next five minutes?' she said, and he felt his shoulders drop about a foot. Thank God. He really, *really* hadn't wanted to think about her in that dangerous annexe with the ceiling coming down round her ears for another night.

His smile widened. 'Sounds good to me.'

He stared at her few meagre possessions in horror. 'Is that all?'

'Most of my clothes got ruined when the ceiling fell in, but it doesn't matter much; they didn't fit me any more. I haven't got much else. I've learned to travel light,' she said.

Light? *Light?* 'I take it the rest of your things are with your mother somewhere?' he said, and she gave a brittle laugh.

'I don't even know where my mother is at the moment,' she said, stuffing a T-shirt into a rucksack. 'Egypt, I think, but I'm not sure. She might be in South America by now—Peru, possibly.'

'So—what about your home?'

She straightened up from the bag and sighed patiently. 'I have no home,' she reminded him. 'I told you that.' She examined a T-shirt, sniffed it and rejected it.

'What—not even a base?' He was appalled, but he reminded himself of what she'd told him about her childhood. Maybe it had been worse than he'd realised. 'You must have some kind of base,' he added, still not able to comprehend what on earth it could be like to belong nowhere.

'Daniel, if I had a base, I wouldn't be living in this hell-hole,' she said reasonably, and he folded his arms, his frown firmly in place, and watched her pack.

If you could call it that. Most of the things were being thrown back on the bed, and he could see the mildew on them.

He swallowed. What an odd, rootless existence. How on earth had she coped? But she couldn't really be surprised if he found it hard to understand her lifestyle. She was the odd one out here, not him.

She tugged the drawcord tight and stood up.

'OK, that's me.'

'Right, let's get you all loaded up and we'll get off.'

They took everything—a rucksack, a battered flight bag and a pair of tired trainers—down to the car, then she straightened up and headed back towards the door.

'I'll just get the cat,' she said blithely, and went back inside.

He followed her. 'Cat? *What* cat?'

'Pebbles. Hotel cat. She'll be about here somewhere. She comes and goes through the window on to the flat roof.'

'So—what's that got to do with you?'

She turned and stared at him in astonishment. 'I feed her.'

'And?' he said, wondering what was coming next and getting a distinct sinking feeling.

'And I can't just leave her. She's old.'

'And if I don't want her in the house?'

'Then I don't come,' she said, quietly but firmly, and he just knew she was crazy enough to mean it.

He sighed and rubbed his hand through his hair. 'Get the cat,' he said, surrendering, and started wandering through the rooms. 'Kitty, kitty, kitty!'

'Save your breath, she's stone deaf. Hence Pebbles. You'll just have to find her—oh, got her!'

And she appeared in the doorway with a scrawny, moth-eaten little tortoiseshell snuggled in her arms.

'Pregnant women should be careful with cats,' he said, and she just laughed at him.

'Don't worry, she's been wormed and she doesn't have a litter tray. Right, that's it. Shall we go?'

He stared at the cat, and she stared back, then turned her head away, dismissing him and snuggling into Iona's arms with a loud and slightly off-key miaow.

Wondering what on earth he'd let himself in for, he gestured to the stairs, and she went down in front of him, got into the car and with one last rattle of the door to make sure it was secure, he got in beside her and started the engine.

'Come on, then, let's go home.'

Home?

Maybe. After the strain of the past few weeks, it seemed like a dream, and she kept expecting to wake up.

He brought her things in through the side door and put them down, her well-used rucksack and flight bag looking horribly shabby in the pristine surroundings of his brand-new and untouched guest suite, and then frowned at the bed.

'I'll give you a hand to make that up, and then I think you should have a shower and a sleep,' he said. 'You look shattered.'

'I'm fine,' she protested. 'I can make the bed, and I need to think about what to cook for you later.'

'No, I'm cooking today. You sort the cat out, I'll get the bedding.'

And no sooner was the bed made than he was gone, leaving her alone with the cat. She had a litter tray now, which he insisted he'd deal with, just until Pebbles was used to the house and could be allowed out; they'd picked it up at the supermarket on the way home, along with some sachets of food, and after christening the litter, eating the food and wandering round for a minute, Pebbles stopped by the bed and miaowed.

Iona sat down on the edge of the bed and sighed. 'Pebbles, I don't know if you're allowed on the bed,' she said softly, but Pebbles couldn't hear her and didn't care, anyway. She miaowed again, her funny, squawky little miaow, and, giving in, Iona picked her up and put her down on the bed.

'No shedding or plucking,' she warned, and felt her eyes drawn to the bathroom door. The lure of hot water was overcoming her, and she went over and looked inside. There were toiletries there, still in a carrier bag—shampoo, conditioner—oh, the luxury!—a toothbrush and toothpaste, flannel—and hanging on the rail were thick fluffy towels that Daniel had brought in with the sheets, and the shower head was the size of a dustbin lid.

Almost moaning with anticipation, she turned on the basin tap and waited a second to see if it ran hot.

Yes! There was real, proper hot water!

Oh, the joy!

She stripped off her clothes, turned on the shower and stood under it motionless for a second, revelling in the sensation of the hot water pummelling down on her. Then she squirted a dollop of shampoo into her hand and worked it up into a lovely rich lather in her hair.

Fabulous. Then conditioner, and gradually it started to feel like hair again instead of straw. There was even a razor on the side! Oh, bliss. She soaped herself gloriously all over, used the razor—such luxury, a new razor!—and then stood rinsing longer than necessary, until guilt began to prick at her and she turned the water off reluctantly and wrapped herself in the towels.

Two towels—one for her body, one for her hair, and a mat for the floor, all pure white and soft as thistledown.

And there was even a hairdryer hard-wired to the wall!

Minutes later, feeling human again and ready for that nap, she pulled a clean T-shirt out of the drawer she'd put it in, sniffed it and wrinkled her nose. It had that horrible smell of washing that had taken too long to dry, and she could hardly bring herself to put it on. She'd wash it—wash all her things—later, if he didn't mind. She was sure he wouldn't. After all, he wouldn't want her smelling of rotten washing.

She sat down on the bed to pull her jeans on, and ran her hand over the bed.

Oh, bliss.

The bedding was so soft and silky it was like a caress against her skin. The quilt felt like goose-down, the mattress was hard enough to be supportive and soft enough to snuggle her, the pillows would be just the right height.

She could snuggle down in it, close her eyes and let go…

Or she could just look at the sea.

The bed was calling her, soft and smooth and inviting, but so was the view, and just now the view was winning, so she went into the sitting room, slid back the door and breathed in the warm summer air.

Gorgeous.

The guest suite—or staff flat, or whatever it was—was set back slightly from the rest of the house, with its own private terrace. It looked clean enough, so she took one of the cushions and sat on it cross-legged on the smooth, warm slate, and resting her hands palm up on her knees, she closed her eyes and let her mind drift.

Sounds.

Birdsong, the soft drag of waves on shingle, cars. A dog barking in the distance, and then from somewhere closer she heard a doorbell.

She tuned them out, breathed deeply and let it

go, but the voices penetrated, angry and frustrated and getting closer, and then she heard the words and shock held her motionless…

'Are you totally insane?'

Emily stalked past him, and Dan shut the door and sighed. 'News travels fast, doesn't it? I take it Georgie's been on the blower.'

'Too right she has—Nick saw you driving away with her earlier, and she said you'd got some cock-eyed notion of making her your housekeeper! What the hell do you think you're doing, taking some aimless drifter into your house? You must be mad!'

Dan followed his sister down the hall and out on to the terrace where she was pacing up and down. 'Solving a problem. I thought you might all be rather grateful—'

'Grateful?' she ranted. 'Because you've lost your marbles?'

'Rubbish. Because I've got our sitting tenant out of the hotel!' he retorted. 'She's was holding things up big-time—and keep your voice down.

She's asleep,' he added belatedly, wondering why Nick hadn't kept his mouth shut, at least until tomorrow. It would have given him a little respite.

But no, Emily was here now, scraping her hair out of her eyes and pacing round the terrace, giving him hell and probably not without justification.

'You're mad,' she said flatly. 'Utterly mad. Harry warned you not to get involved, but you didn't listen. I might have known you'd pull a crazy stunt like this.'

He pulled the door to, so their voices didn't drift down the hall to Iona. 'Em, she's pregnant. The ceiling had fallen in. How the hell could I leave her there?'

'Oh, I've got no problem with that—it's bringing her here and installing her in your house—'

'Like that's so unprecedented,' he said drily.

Emily gave a low growl under her breath and skewered him with an icy glare. 'Well, exactly! You're just as gullible as Harry. What is it with you bloody men and pregnant women? You fall for it every time.'

'Oh, come on, Em, this isn't Carmen, and I've

got no intention of marrying her. We aren't
talking about a pregnant teenager who'd been
raped. Iona's an adult, she's made a conscious
decision to keep her baby, she's clever—'

'Clever enough to outwit you, evidently! She's
a drifter, Dan—a rootless bit of flotsam that's
drifted up on the shores of Yoxburgh!'

'Actually, no. She's an educated, intelligent,
mature, funny, brave cosmopolitan woman—she
was reading law at Maastricht! And *she* doesn't
have a closed mind,' he added pointedly.

'So she's a graduate?'

Damn. 'No. She didn't finish uni. Her
mother was sick—'

'How convenient. So she's not just a drifting
backpacker, she's a bright and articulate
drifting backpacker and sees this as a way of
making money off the back of an executor's
sale—she was probably working on him to
change his will, and he got there before her
and popped his clogs!'

He hung on to his patience with difficulty.
'No, she was looking after him because his own

sons wouldn't! And apparently before he died he was making plans to secure her daughter's future!' he told her.

'I'll just bet he was. So where's the will?'

'That's what everybody wants to know.'

Emily rolled her eyes and sighed impatiently. 'And in the meantime she's trying to get the other brother, Ian, to cough up. Good grief, I can't believe you men are all so gullible! She's a conniving shark, Daniel! Why can't you see it?'

'Because I don't think it's true—and even if it was, if she's doing it to secure her daughter's future, what's so wrong with that? Carmen married Harry for that reason, and as a result Kizzy's secure, she's loved and she has a good future.'

'Only because I was able to help Harry to look after her when Carmen died, but I'm not helping you to get yourself into the same mess, because I've seen what it's done to Harry, and it's nearly torn him apart. He still blames himself for her death.'

'That's ridiculous,' he said flatly, frowning. 'She's dead because she didn't look before she crossed the road. It's not his fault—but if I'd left Iona in the hotel and the roof had fallen in, it would have been my fault. And I don't want that on my conscience, and you shouldn't, either. Nor should Harry or Nick or Georgie. Anyway, I would have thought you'd be glad she was out. At least this way we can get on with demolishing that wing and getting the building work back on schedule. We aren't running a charity here, and I need to see a return on that investment, and so do you guys.'

Emily gave a short sigh and scraped her hair back again. 'You're going to end up in so much trouble,' she grumbled. 'I can see it now. You'll end up involved with her—knowing you, you'll fall in love with her, and she'll screw you over just like Kate did.'

'Leave Kate out of this!' he growled. 'This is nothing to do with Kate.'

'No, it's to do with you, and your lousy judgement of character and naïve inability to see the worst in people. Well, when she takes you to the cleaners—slaps a harassment suit on you, or some trumped-up rape charge, don't tell me you weren't warned!'

'Rubbish, you're being ridiculous! I have no intention of getting involved with her. She's pregnant with someone else's baby, and anyway, I couldn't be less interested in her,' he lied, and ignored the little jab from his conscience. 'The housekeeping thing is just a way of getting her out of the hotel, and if she's any good, so much the better. It'll kill two birds with one stone—three if you count getting the baby somewhere safer, which I'm sure you do, being the soft-hearted woman you are.'

'Don't bet on it,' she said, and levelled a finger at Dan. 'And on the subject of this baby, how do you know it's the brother's at all? It could be the chef's or some other random—'

'You haven't even met her,' Dan retorted, cutting her off, 'and you talk about me being a lousy judge of character? At least I've met the girl to *judge* her. For God's sake, she was going to be a human rights lawyer!'

'Nice line. Pity you fell for it. When did she tell you that?'

'In the half-hour I spent getting to know her yesterday,' he retorted. 'Which is more than you've done. And anyway, when did you get to be so cynical and bitter?'

'When Pete walked out on me because he wasn't interested in his own children!' Her voice changed, softening, and he could see the worry in her eyes. 'Dan, please, be careful. She could be a perfect saint for all we know, but what if she isn't? What if she's some twisted, money-grubbing little bitch? I don't think I can bear to watch this.'

'Then don't. I'm prepared to take the risk, because I believe her, but if it makes you happy, I'll get a contract of employment drawn up tomorrow while we're talking to the legal team about her,' he said, going back to the kitchen and the onions he'd been chopping when she'd arrived. 'And now, if you don't mind, I have things to do.'

'Yeah, like cooking for your housekeeper,' she said, her voice ripe with disbelief. 'And I thought I was a sucker!' She rummaged in her bag for her keys and shook her head. 'Just be careful, eh? You're taking a hell of a risk.'

'What about her? She's vulnerable, Em. So vulnerable, so desperate that she's prepared to take a job living in the house of a total stranger, a single man about whom she knows *nothing*. I could be a rapist, a paedophile—anything. She's spoken to Georgie, that's all. How the hell would Georgie know if I have a dirty little secret life? I could be any one of those things, and she wouldn't know. Nobody would know. So how about thinking of it from her perspective? How would you feel in her situation?'

'You're forgetting—I've *been* in her situation.'

He shook his head. 'No, you haven't. When Pete left you pregnant and alone, Mum and Dad were there for you. But what if they hadn't been? What would have happened to you? Em, for God's sake, she's got no one. This isn't her fault. And she reminds me so much of you—'

'OK, OK, I give up,' she said and, throwing Dan a frustrated smile, she headed for the door. 'Just don't say I didn't warn you. I'll see you tomorrow—if she hasn't murdered you in your bed. And lock up your wallet.'

'Yes, Mummy.'

She stuck her tongue out and went, and Dan walked out into the garden and stared out over the sea while he calmed down. The water was choppy now, the sky suddenly dark and menacing, and in the distance he heard the rumble of thunder. There was a band of rain moving in across the water, and it would hit them any time now. Thank God Iona was out of that leaky annexe—whatever Emily and the rest of them had to say on the subject.

He glanced over towards the guest suite and wondered if she was still asleep. Probably. She'd looked exhausted. He'd leave her until she woke up naturally. He could finish the cooking when she got up and came and found him, and they'd eat together. He realised he was looking forward to it.

Emily's words rang in his ears, but he ignored them, as he'd ignored Harry's warning. Harry and Emily hadn't met her. They had no idea what she was like, and Dan had absolutely no intention of getting personally involved with her.

It would just be nice to have a little company, that was all.

The rain arrived, slashing, horizontal sheets racing towards him, bending the trees and shrubs before it, and he went back inside and shut the door just before it thrashed against the glass. He glanced at his watch.

Four o'clock. He was getting hungry. He hadn't had lunch, and breakfast had been disgustingly early.

He found some biscuits, made a cup of tea and went through to his studio, leaving the door open so he could hear her when she woke. With any luck it wouldn't be long…

He'd lied to her!

All that rubbish about needing a housekeeper. He was one of them! One of the developers who'd wanted her out. He'd lied to her—lied and cheated and tricked her, and his sister had the gall—the *gall*!—to suggest that *she* couldn't be trusted? How *dared* she! How dared any of them?

She was going to be sick.

Heart pounding, nausea rising in her throat and her legs barely able to support her weight, Iona grabbed her few miserable possessions and stuffed them in her rucksack and the ancient flight bag that carried everything of any importance to her.

Except her pride, and right now that was in tatters.

She'd *known* it was too good to be true! Had known it was all going to come crashing down around her sooner or later. Well, it had—in spades. Just rather quicker than she'd imagined. Still, at least she'd had a shower and washed her hair, and it was just as well she hadn't had time to get too used to it. She could go back to being a *drifter* right now!

'Come on, Pebbles,' she whispered, scooping her up, and opening the other door a crack into her little hall, the one which led to the drive, she listened carefully for any sound before she opened the door a fraction further and scanned the front garden.

She froze at the sound of a door opening, but then it closed and she heard the slap of flip-flops.

She peeped carefully through the gap. A woman was getting into a car, dressed in jeans and a T-shirt and the flip-flops. So that was Emily. Taller than her, maybe a size larger, a little older perhaps. She looked harmless, but she'd heard her voice—and her words and Dan's were ringing in her ears, sickening her.

Where was Dan? She'd heard the front door shut, and Emily hadn't looked back or waved, so she thought it was probably safe. And if she didn't hurry, she'd miss the electric gates.

Damn. She hadn't thought of that. Shrugging the rucksack on to one shoulder and cramming a couple of sachets of cat food into her flight bag as an afterthought, she crept out into the front garden, looked around and hurried after the car. The drive was empty, and the gates were starting to swing shut, so she sprinted through them with inches to spare, then paused on the pavement and scanned the road each side.

Nothing. Emily must have turned off.

Good.

She realised she was crying, and she wanted to

scrub the angry tears off her cheeks, but her hands were full of bags and cat, so she wiped them ineffectually against her shoulders and set course for the hotel. It wasn't far—maybe half a mile at the most? She could do that. Of course she could—even on shaking legs. And then she could fall apart in private.

It took her only fifteen minutes, and as she turned the corner, her composure hanging by a thread, she was stopped in her tracks by the sight of a workman fixing a sheet of board over her door.

The cry of protest stuck in her throat.

Her bolt-hole was gone, her retreat cut off. Dismal as it had been, she'd hung on to the illusion of safety it had represented, but now even that had been taken away from her.

She'd lost everything—her home, her right to stay there, the only lever she'd had in her claim against Ian for her baby's birthright. All gone at a stroke, and the job she'd foolishly hoped would be her passport out of there wasn't worth the paper it was written on.

She laughed. What was she thinking? She didn't even have a bit of paper with it written on!

She had nothing.

And then, right on cue, as if things weren't already bad enough, the wind whipped up and an icy squall drenched her to the skin…

CHAPTER FOUR

WHERE on earth was she?

It was almost dark outside, the rain still lashing against the glass, and Dan couldn't believe she hadn't appeared yet. She hadn't seemed *that* tired, and he would have thought the thunder and lightning would have woken her.

He glanced at his watch and frowned. Eight-thirty, just gone. Was she really still sleeping? Maybe she was waiting in her room, reading or something, expecting him to call her. What had he said to do? He couldn't remember his exact words. Had it been ambiguous?

He went down the hall to the entrance to the guest suite, and tapped on the door. 'Iona?'

There was no reply, so he eased the door open

and was greeted by a blast of fresh air. He frowned. How strange. The outside door leading to the drive swung to with a crash as he came in, and the door from the sitting room to the garden was wide open, the rain driving in. He called her again, louder this time, but there was no reply. There was a cushion on the paving outside, getting soaked.

Why? He went out on to the terrace and picked it up, then glanced across at the other terrace to his right. The terrace where he and Emily had been talking.

About Iona.

He felt a sickening sense of dread. If she'd heard them...

She might not have done. He went back in out of the rain and shut the sliding door, then called again, then went through to the bedroom and stopped dead.

Empty. The whole flat was completely empty, except for the cat's litter tray and the food bowls. Her bags were gone, the cat was gone—Iona was gone, and with hideous certainty, he knew why.

He groaned and leant back against the wall, staring up at the ceiling. She'd heard them. She must have heard them. She must have been sitting out there on the cushion and overheard Emily giving him an earful.

Overheard all of it. She would have realised that he was one of the developers, thought that he'd wanted her out for commercial reasons— misunderstood his motives and, instead of confronting him, she'd run.

Oh, hell. She'd be back in that terrible annexe again, holed up like a criminal in the stinking, crumbling ruin that should have had a closure order on it! And no way was she going to let him talk her out of there again.

But he had to try. He couldn't just leave her there without trying to explain, and at the very least he had to pay for her to go into a hotel.

'I'm going to kill you, Emily,' he growled under his breath, and shutting the side door and locking it, he ran back through the house, grabbed his keys, punched in the alarm code and went out. His car was still outside, and he got into it and gunned it down the drive, paused impatiently while the gates opened and then stared at them.

How would she have got out of the gates? He hadn't had time to show her where the keypad was, and she didn't know the code anyway. So was she still here, in the grounds, waiting for the gates to open, or had she left when Emily did? Hours ago—hell, nearly five hours ago, and the storm had been raging ever since.

No. She'd gone. She must have done, he thought, but he searched the gardens anyway, just to be certain.

No trace.

He left the gates open in case she came back, and drove slowly to the hotel, scouring the shadows for any sign of her, his heart pounding even though he knew she wasn't there. She must have left right after Emily, must be there by now, safely locked away under those collapsing ceilings.

He swore softly under his breath, craning his neck to see, and then turned the corner to the hotel and braked to a halt.

The door was boarded up! Nick must have got

on to it the moment he'd known she was out, because of the danger. He'd said he was worried about the public liability angle. He must have got one of the building team to secure it straight away.

And now he had no idea where to find her.

He stared around through the streaming windows, and felt fear for her grip him. She'd be freezing, for all it was June. Freezing and angry and betrayed and all alone.

No, not alone. She had the cat, the poor, ancient, moth-eaten little cat that she'd refused to leave.

Damn!

He slammed his hand on the steering-wheel and growled.

What now? He punched in Emily's number, fear and anger pushing him over the brink.

'Iona's disappeared. She must have heard us talking. Get out there and look for her—and I don't want any damned excuses. This is your fault. You came bursting into my house making unfounded accusations against a person you'd never even met, and if any harm comes to her, I'll hold you personally responsible.'

'Oh, Dan, no! It's vile out there! Where are you now?'

'Outside the hotel. The annexe door's been boarded up. She's got nowhere to go, so she might have gone back to my house. Get round there and search the garden again. I only had a quick look. I've left the gate open, but the house is locked so she might be sheltering somewhere in the garden, at the back of the shrubbery or somewhere.'

'No, she won't be out in the open, Dan, not in this storm! It's filthy out there!'

'I've noticed—and I've no doubt that she has, too, after five hours. And I'm hoping she might have had the sense to come back to the house.'

'Really?' she said skeptically. 'Is that likely?'

He rubbed a hand through his hair. 'Probably not, after what she must have heard, but she doesn't have a lot of options, I don't think. Just do it, Em, or send Harry, and if you don't find her, then drive round and round looking until you do, and I'll do the same round this area. And call me!'

'Hang on! I don't know what she looks like!'

Beautiful.

He cleared his throat, his voice sharper than he'd intended when he spoke. 'Yeah, you do. A pregnant woman with a rucksack and a cat. There won't be many of them. If anything's happened to her, I might just have to kill you.'

He jabbed the phone, cutting her off, and dialled Nick. 'Get out in the car and start looking for Iona. She's disappeared,' he said, and filled him in, giving him the same pithy description he'd given Emily.

'I'm on it,' he said, and the line went dead.

She was so cold.

Her teeth were chattering, she was soaked right through to the skin and on her lap Pebbles was shaking. The cat might be deaf, but she could feel the thunder, and the poor little thing was terrified. They were huddled in a doorway by the side of a shop, the doorway Daniel had dragged her into—gracious, was it really only last night? It was round the other side of the hotel from the annexe where she'd been living, and at least it was a little sheltered from the rain, but it was a busier road, and people kept looking at her.

None of them stopped, too busy trying to get home out of the rain, and frankly she was quite grateful for that, because she didn't want to have to move or explain herself. She and the cat were at least sheltered there, and sitting on her rucksack she was reasonably comfortable. Well, that was probably pushing it, but comfort was the least of her worries at the moment.

Where to go next was much more pressing, and with the cat in tow her choices were frankly hugely limited.

What was she thinking? Her choices were negligible anyway, what with having no funds, no friends in the area and probably a good few enemies.

Not least Emily, who for some reason seemed to have a real hatred of her, even though she'd never met her. Something to do with Harry—her husband?—and someone called Carmen, but she hadn't caught it all. And Kate, whoever she was.

Not that it mattered. Nothing mattered except finding somewhere dry where she could lie down, because she was beginning to change her priorities about the comfort thing.

She looked up, wondering if there was anywhere she could sit for a while in the station opposite and get a bit warmer, and there right in front of her was Daniel's car, cruising slowly down the street.

Dear God, he was looking for her! She didn't need this now. Not at the moment, when she was so cold and angry she was likely to say something that would land her in court. She shrank back into the opening, trying to make herself invisible, but it was hopeless. He'd seen her. He swung the wheel, hitched the car up on the kerb and jumped out, leaving the engine running and the door hanging open into the road.

Horns tooted, but he ignored them and ran over to her, crouching down in the doorway so she couldn't see his face. She could hear him, though, hear the tremor in his voice as he gripped her arm and shook it lightly.

'Where the hell have you been? I've been worried out of my mind!'

'Let go of me,' she said clearly, and he dropped her as if he'd suddenly realised what he was doing.

'I'm sorry—Iona, please, come and sit in the car and talk to me. Let me explain.'

'No. I'm not coming with you.'

'I'll give you the keys. That way I can't drive you anywhere you don't want to go. But please let me explain.' He jammed his hand through his hair and water flew from the strands. She looked at him more closely and realised he was soaked. Soaked to the skin and nearly as cold as she was. He'd been out looking for her, she realised, not just in the car, but walking up and down, searching for her in the pouring rain.

But why?

'Explain what?' she asked, her voice curiously flat considering her turbulent emotions. 'Why you lied to me?'

He sighed a little raggedly. 'I didn't lie. I just didn't tell you all the truth.'

She laughed at that, at the absolute absurdity

of it. 'All? How about you didn't tell me most of it? Or at least the bit that mattered.'

'I did tell you the bit that mattered,' he said, and his voice was strangely sincere and subdued.

A car horn honked, and there was a screech of brakes.

'You've left your door open,' she reminded him unnecessarily, but he didn't budge.

'Please. Come with me. Let's go somewhere you can get warm and have something hot to eat and drink, and talk about this. We'll go somewhere public—a café or something. You can choose.'

'I've got the cat,' she pointed out, and he sighed.

'Iona, please,' he said again, and because he wasn't moving, because he was starting to shiver and he was getting even wetter, if that were possible, she relented.

'OK, but just in the car. We aren't going anywhere. And you've got five minutes.'

He had to move the car. It was obstructing the traffic, but he just drove round the corner, turned into the hotel car park and pulled up next to the skip containing her old mattress. Then he cut the engine, handed her the keys and shifted so he was facing her.

'I don't know where to start apologising,' he said, knowing he could blow this so easily and drive her back out into the rain.

'Cut the apologies. I want the truth—all of it. And can you put the heater on?'

'Not without the keys.'

She handed them back without a word, and he started the engine and cranked the heating up. They were so wet that even with the climate control on, the windows started to steam up, and there was a definite smell of wet dog and nasty washing. And the cat was shaking.

Poor old Pebbles.

Iona was stroking her, her fingers almost blue with cold, and she needed to get out of those wet clothes.

'This is crazy. Please let me take you home and get you dry and give you something to eat. You must be starving, and you're so cold, and the cat's freezing.'

She looked down at Pebbles, and something dripped on her. It could have been water from her hair, but it could equally have been a tear, and his heart twisted.

He reached out his hand and touched her cheek, turning her to face him, and saw another tear sliding down her proud, angry face.

He brushed it away with his thumb, then met her stubborn grey eyes—beautiful eyes, like a rainwashed sky, wary and defensive and defiant to the last. And disappointed. In him. That hurt.

He swallowed. 'Please let me take you home. You don't have to stay. I'll leave the gates open, you can go whenever you like. I won't hurt you, Iona.'

'No. You'll just lie to me, you and your sister and your friends. I thought I was fighting Ian, but you were the real enemy all the time, and now I'm out and you've won. Well, congratulations. How does it feel, stealing from a baby?' She knocked his hand away, scrubbing furiously at the tears that somehow wouldn't stop falling.

'We haven't—'

'Oh, you have! It's hers, Daniel! She should have her inheritance, and now I'm out it'll be so much harder. I knew it was stupid letting you talk me into leaving, but you were so damn convincing, you and your friends, and it was all just a pack of lies, a way of getting me out. I *knew* it was too good to be true. I even told you that, and still I fell for it. I can't believe I was so *stupid*! But you shouldn't have had the door boarded up. I could have gone back there. I still could. I'll unscrew it—'

'No.' He shook his head. 'It's too dangerous,' he said, and as if to illustrate his point, a sheet of roofing material blew off the flat roof in front of them and tumbled across the car park, coming to rest against the skip.

Her lip wobbled, and she bit it and turned her head away, just as the phone rang. He turned it on, on hands-free so she could hear what Emily had to say.

'Any news?'

'I've got her,' he told his sister, and there was a heartfelt sigh.

'Thank God,' she said, her voice relieved. 'Is she OK?'

'No thanks to you.'

'Oh, Dan, don't, I'm kicking myself. I'm so, so sorry. It's just the Carmen thing—I could see you getting sucked in and I know what you guys are like when you get all protective. It's too close to home for me, and I'm sorry I threw Kate in your face, that was uncalled for. Look, I'll come round, talk to her, explain—'

'I think you've said quite enough today,' he told her. 'Don't worry, I'm looking after her.'

There was a tiny pause, then Emily said, 'Right. Um—tell her I'm sorry, will you? And I'll give you a call tomorrow.'

'Do that.'

He cut off the phone, and turned to her. 'I need to ring Nick. He's out looking for you too.'

'Worried about a lawsuit?'

He gave a harsh sigh and ran his fingers through his wet hair. 'No. He's worried about a vulnerable young woman out on the street in a thunderstorm, with nowhere to go because of his actions.' He took a breath and softened his voice. 'We aren't out to get you, Iona. We're on your side.'

She snorted. 'Well, forgive me if I don't quite believe you,' she said tautly, and then her anger at Emily came rushing to the fore again. 'How dare she, Dan? How *dare* she make those accusations about me? She's never even *met* me! I don't care if she is your sister, it's just unforgivable. I would *never* make snap judgements like that about anyone. Who does she think she *is*?'

She realised she was talking pretty much in italics, and snapped her mouth shut, turning to look out of the window. Not that she could see through it in the pouring rain, but it beat looking at Daniel and wondering if he was a genuinely nice man or just a gullible sucker like his sister said. Or worse. As he'd pointed out, Georgie didn't know what he got up to in his private life. Maybe he was a serial sex offender?

She was about to get out of the car and head off into the rain again when there was an almighty flash and clap of thunder right near them, and the cat shivered and cried out. No. She couldn't do it. Pebbles would die, and she couldn't have that on her conscience.

Daniel was ringing Nick, telling him Iona was safe, saying he'd speak to him in the morning. She was treated to Nick's apology, too, before Daniel cut him off, and maybe it was that, or maybe it was just the cold and the fact that Pebbles was crying pitifully now, but she turned to him, her chin stuck out in that way he was beginning to find rather familiar.

'OK,' she said, her voice like ice. 'But just because of the cat. I'll let you take me back so I can get her dry and feed her, and I'll change, and I want to know exactly what's going on. Then we'll talk about me staying.'

He gave a silent sigh of relief and nodded. 'OK.'

'Where do you want me to start?'

She eyed him warily, not sure she could believe a word that came out of his beautiful lying mouth, but he'd left the gates open, had shown her where the keypad was and told her what the combination was that would open them if they were shut at any time.

He'd also given her a key to the front door and the side door, the code for the burglar alarm, and cash, nearly two hundred pounds, all he had on him, he'd said. And a cash card and his pin.

Really? So trusting? She wouldn't have been. Maybe his sister was right about him. Or maybe it was because even if she went mad with his cash card, it couldn't rival the damage to their commercial enterprise of her squatting in the hotel annexe and holding up their purchase. So—damage limitation, or genuinely decent? The jury was still out.

He'd shooed her into the guest suite, and by the time she'd come out of the shower he'd wrapped the cat in a warm towel and fed her, and unpacked her bag.

'Your clothes are soaked,' he said, frowning, and left her, coming back a minute later with a pair of jog bottoms, a T-shirt and a big fluffy towelling robe that she snuggled into gratefully. They were all far too big for her, but she didn't care; she was warm, and the cat was on her lap, sleeping, her clothes were in the washing machine and she was waiting for him to begin.

He must have showered at some point—probably while she'd dressed—and he was wearing worn old jeans and a soft cotton jumper. His feet were encased in thick sports socks, and he propped them up on the coffee table between them and met her eyes.

'Start at the beginning,' she said. 'When you first realised I was living there, and you decided to hatch this plot.'

'It's not a plot.'

'What would you call it, then? Oh, yes, I remember—"solving a problem",' she said, her voice putting it in quotes. 'I think those were your words, pretty much.'

He swore softly and rubbed his hands through his hair, ruffling the damp strands and perversely, crazily, making her fingers itch to straighten it out, to lift that lock that had fallen over his forehead and ease it back out of the way so she could see his eyes better.

But he lifted his head, so she could see them anyway, and she let her fingers stroke the cat, instead. Much safer, and much, much more sensible.

'It was about a fortnight after we completed—'

'Completed?' she said, sitting bolt upright and staring at him in horror.

'Yes—what, did you think we were just wasting legal fees and making your life a misery for the sake of it? Of course we've completed. We completed the day before Brian died. We'd made an agreement that he could stay there for up to a month after completion to give him time to clear his debts and find somewhere to live, but to be honest I think he realised he was dying and he wanted the money in the bank before then, so the sale wasn't compromised, so he let us rush it through.'

'And he died before he could do anything with it,' she said softly, sinking back against the sofa, her mind whirling. 'But if you've paid the money—then where is it? Does Ian have it?'

'No, I don't imagine so. The probate office

won't release it until probate's been granted. There was a small retention, to be paid over when the property was finally handed over with vacant possession, and we've still got that, because of course we haven't had vacant possession until today.'

'Until you engineered my move.'

He sighed tiredly. 'I didn't engineer your move—well, that's a lie, I did, I suppose, but not for that reason.'

'Why, then?' she challenged.

'Because it was so dangerous! I didn't sleep last night for worrying about you under that ceiling, and rightly, because when I came back this morning the chunk over the stairs was down. The roof's in shreds, Iona. You saw that sheet of felt fly off it. The boards will be rotten, and probably the joists. It's only a matter of time before the lot falls in. And there's the baby to think about.'

She looked down, her hands instinctively curving around her daughter. He was right, it had been dangerous. Last night when the hall ceiling fell down had been scary, but she'd been in the bathroom when the ceiling had come down in the bedroom a week ago, and the potential consequences of that had been even more terrifying. All her clothes had been ruined, the mattress soaked and covered in plaster, the room all but destroyed.

If she'd been in the bed—

She shuddered, and a quick frown flickered across his face. 'Are you all right? Warm enough?'

She squared her shoulders. 'Yes,' she said, although she was very far from all right even if she was warm now, and as if he knew that, he sighed. After a long pause, he spoke again.

'Iona, I know what it must look like, but I really wanted you out of there for the best possible reasons, and if it also suited us that you were no longer in the building, that was just a bonus. If it had been safe, I would have left you there if that was what you wanted and then taken you to see our legal team tomorrow to talk through your claim.'

'So you can sort it out and get rid of me in the shortest possible time?'

'Because I don't want to see you cheated by a man who couldn't even be bothered to visit his sick father until he was dying,' he said tightly.

Could she believe him? He sounded angry enough.

She sighed. She didn't really have an option, she thought. She had nowhere to live, no money to live off and a baby on the way. Soon. She didn't have the luxury of multiple choices, and she was so tired of fighting.

'You know, if I'd realised that you'd completed, that whatever I did couldn't stop the money from changing hands, I needn't have spent all that time there in that horrible place,' she said heavily. 'I thought it was all held up by probate—so why didn't you just get me chucked out?'

He chuckled, to her surprise. 'We have been trying,' he pointed out. 'That's why we were seeing the law team tomorrow. We were still having difficulty evicting you, and then there was the question of your safety and our public liability to add to it,' he said. 'We're going to demolish that wing, and you were seriously holding up our schedule. We'd got a meeting lined up for tomorrow with the legal team to discuss it.'

'So why did you offer me the job? I mean, if your hotshot team were about to pull out the big guns, why not just let them get on with it now?'

His eyes flicked away, and he looked a little uncomfortable. 'Because we found out you're pregnant,' he said, pointing out the obvious.

'So?'

He looked shocked. 'So, it makes a difference. A huge difference. My sister ended up in a similar situation when she was pregnant, and she came home to live with our parents. She was a little older than you, with a small daughter and another baby on the way, but at least she had our family home to run to. You have nowhere, and however much a bastard you might think me, I couldn't just turn you out onto the street. And I didn't think you'd accept charity, and you have to admit I could use someone to help me keep this place in order. And it's not like I'm short of space.'

She couldn't argue with that, but there was something about the way he wouldn't look at her that made her wonder about his motivation. Something he was hiding from her, or at least not ready to share. Something to do with Kate? Whatever. She'd come back to it later.

'So how exactly did you find out about me?' she asked. 'At the beginning?'

'We were told there was a sitting tenant— some person who'd been working in the hotel and was making some ridiculous claim—his words, not mine—on the property. They said it wasn't a problem, you'd be moving out within the month. And then the month was over, and you were still there.'

'And Ian told you I didn't have a claim?'

'That's right. Or his solicitors did—although how they could say that without the will, I have no idea.'

'Even without it, there's a chance I can claim for her. There's an ancient piece of legislation in-volving babies—*en ventre sa mère*.'

He nodded, and she searched his eyes, surprised. It was a pretty obscure thing. Had he been scouring the net?

'I have to be able to prove that she's Jamie's, though, before I can do anything—'

'Is there any question?'

She glared at him, and he just raised his hands. 'Only asking, Iona. It could be relevant. If you only think it's Jamie's, we need to know if we're footing the bill.'

'Does mistrust run in the family?' she asked, and he winced. Actually, even she winced at the harshness of her tone, and she softened it, relenting. 'She's Jamie's. Of course she is. It's not me who needs the proof, Dan,' she added more gently. 'It's the courts. And if Ian gets the money before she's born—'

'But he won't get it. He won't have it yet, and if you make a claim, probate won't be granted until they've proved it one way or another. Our solicitors will go over it with you tomorrow and start things moving—assuming you'll talk to them?'

She was back to that whole choice thing, and it was pretty cut and dried. Go out on the streets and throw herself on the mercy of the local housing department, and try and fight a legal battle without funding—because she couldn't get legal aid for this, she'd checked, and she had no intention of using one of those unscrupulous 'no claim, no fee' firms that advertised all over the place—or she could stay here, in this beautiful, peaceful, sublime house, with a man who, despite her misgivings and the fact that he had no reason to trust her, had been nothing but kind to her, and let him help her fight her legal battle from a position of security.

And that was the word that did it for her.

Security.

For her, and for the cat, and most particularly for her daughter.

'Iona?'

She met his eyes—gentle, concerned—and tried to smile.

'I'm sorry. I think I might have misjudged you. I probably owe you the benefit of the doubt, at least.'

'I think, in view of what you heard, it would

have been quite reasonable if you did misjudge me,' he said, his mouth kicking up in a rueful smile. Then his smile faded, and his brow creased into a frown. 'So—can you forgive me? Forgive us? And will you stay?'

She thought about it. They maybe had a little way to go yet before she could forgive him, and she'd have to think long and hard about forgiving Emily, but stay? Maybe. 'You said something about an employment contract. I think that would be a good idea—put it on a proper footing. I don't want anybody making insinuations.'

He nodded. 'Of course. We can do that tomorrow.'

'And you mentioned supper,' she added, and the frown vanished, replaced by a smile that warmed her battered, exhausted heart.

'I did,' he said. 'A chicken casserole—it's all ready in the oven.'

She returned his smile cautiously. 'Then let's start there—and we'll worry about the rest tomorrow.'

CHAPTER FIVE

THEY made it through to the morning.

Iona without running away again, and Daniel without lying awake all night and wondering if she was still there.

He'd contemplated setting the burglar alarm so if she opened the outer door it would go off, but he'd thought better of it. He didn't want her feeling trapped, and he had to trust her.

She'd said she'd stay. So he gave her the benefit of the doubt, and in the morning, she was still there.

He knew that because when he got out of bed he saw her standing motionless at the end of the garden, swathed almost from head to toe in his towelling robe and looking out over the calm, tranquil sea, and he felt a welling of something he really didn't want to analyse pushing up through his chest.

He pressed the button to cloud the windows, something he never usually did, and after showering and dressing, he went downstairs to put the kettle on and saw her still standing there, her face tipped up slightly to the sky, soaking it up. He slid the door open and stepped out on to the terrace, and she turned and smiled, the sunlight glinting in her hair.

'Morning,' he said, and she headed back towards the house, her feet bare in the wet grass.

'Morning. I was just soaking up the sea air.'

'You'll be there a while, then,' he said, unable to keep the smile in check, and she smiled back.

'I'll take the risk. It's worth it. It's beautiful here.'

'Did you sleep well?'

She nodded. 'I was tired.'

'Hard day yesterday.'

'Yes.' She said no more, but there was a lingering reserve in her eyes that hadn't been there at first, and it saddened him. 'How enclosed is the garden?' she asked instead after a pause.

'Completely.'

'So would Pebbles be able to get out if I let her out of the house?'

'Only if the gates were open, and they aren't usually. And if you let her into the back garden, she can't get round to the front. I take it she can't climb? There's a wall with a door in it up by the garage, and another wall on the other side, and she can't get down to the beach unless the gate's unlocked.'

'So she could go out through the sitting room door and walk round the garden?'

'She could.'

Iona smiled. 'She'd love that. She used to lie on the roof in the sun for hours and watch the birds; she's probably long past being able to catch anything, but she'd love to see them.'

'I'm sure. Let her out, by all means. It would do her good to stretch her legs.'

Her smile widened and she went, leaving wet footprints on the slate, and he heard her door slide open and waited for her to emerge with the cat. It took a minute, but then finally Pebbles appeared at her side, looking round cautiously, ready to run if anything threatening appeared.

'Tea or coffee?' he asked, and she looked up.

'Tea would be lovely, but aren't I meant to be making it?'

'Only if you're taking the job.'

The pause stretched out forever, until he thought he'd probably blown it, but then she smiled and said, 'I'll make the tea,' and he let out the breath he hadn't known he was holding and grinned back.

'You watch the cat. I'm not sure early morning tea should be in your job description anyway,' he said, and went back inside, humming cheerfully to himself and not allowing himself to consider why he should suddenly feel so damned happy.

'What time's our appointment with the solicitors?'

He frowned. 'Not sure. Ten?'

'Oh.' She looked at the clock and chewed her lip. She'd really meant to go through her clothes last night and sort out something to wear, but what with all the upset—

'What's wrong?'

'My clothes all stink—well, such as they are. I was going to wash them last night. I can't really go to the solicitors in my tatty jeans and that T-shirt.'

The memory of the previous evening's events shadowed his eyes, and he frowned. 'Have you got any maternity clothes?' he asked.

'Baggy sweatpants, a few T-shirts. Nothing respectable, really. My jeans don't fit any more, but they're the best thing I've got and at least they were washed last night, thanks to you.'

The frown deepened, and he ran his eyes over her assessingly. Since she was still wearing his big towelling robe with her bare feet sticking out the bottom, she felt a little self-conscious. She pulled it tighter.

'I could ask Emily if she's got anything.'

She swallowed and felt her chin come up a notch. 'Please don't bother. I'll wear my jeans.'

He dragged a hand through his hair and sighed. 'Look, we'll go shopping straight afterwards, OK? Get you something.'

'And that'll really help with the money-grubbing bitch thing,' she muttered under her breath.

'Rubbish,' he said, his hearing obviously acute enough to catch her words. 'Think of it as uniform.'

She didn't say a word, but her face must have given her away, because he chuckled. 'Not the French maid variety,' he said drily. 'But you need clothes if you're going to help me to entertain. After all, you can hardly hide in the kitchen, can you? And anyway, the ceiling was our responsibility, so technically you could look on it as claiming off us for replacements.'

Logical. And clever of him, and a get-out clause for her pride, on the clothes front, although she panicked a little about the entertaining thing. Entertaining who, for instance? Hopefully not his sister. But he was studying her, waiting for her answer, and she let it go for now.

'Just a few things,' she conceded. 'Just until I've earned enough to buy more.'

He nodded. 'Done. Right, we ought to get on. I'd like to leave in half an hour—is that enough time for you to get ready?'

She nearly laughed out loud. It would take her two minutes to do what she could do, or days, if she was going to do it properly—the haircut, the new clothes, shoes that weren't flip-flops or dropping to pieces, a facial, make-up—the list went on and on, but that was for later. It seemed everything was for later.

'Half an hour's plenty,' she assured him, and used the time to put her clothes into the washing machine. She was only going to let him buy her a few things. The rest would have to do for now.

They set off for the solicitors right on time, and as they walked into the office, two men got to their feet and came over. Harry and Nick, she realised. She recognised Harry from the television reports that he used to present from all over the world, but Nick's face was also slightly familiar. She realised she'd seen him around the hotel before Brian died, only she'd never realised his significance.

They looked sober, she thought, and a little uncomfortable in her presence—Harry, particularly, presumably because it was his wife who'd upset her last night. She put it behind her, straightened her shoulders and went over to them, hand outstretched.

'Hi, I'm Iona Lockwood,' she said, and made herself meet Harry's eyes.

He shook her hand. 'Harry Kavenagh,' he said. 'I have instructions from Emily to apologise to you on her behalf.'

She found a smile. She wasn't even slightly sure that Emily had said any such thing, but she gave him credit for doing it for her. Although she had apologised to Dan on the phone last night, and she'd wanted to come over, so maybe—

'Nick Barron,' the other man said, and smiled at her as he shook her hand. 'I recognise you. You were working on Reception when I met Brian Dawes.'

'Reception and everywhere else,' she said ruefully. 'It's a good job I can multi-task.'

They chuckled, and the atmosphere eased a little. They were called in then, and the solicitor was very interested to hear her story, so she told it again.

'And you say there's no sign of the will, Miss Lockwood?'

'Not that Ian could find, and I don't know where Brian would have put it.'

'Did he have a solicitor?'

'I don't know. There was a man—Barry Edwards, I think his name was. He might have known something about it. He was dealing with the sale, I think, but I don't know where he was from. Brian kept it very much to himself.'

'I know Barry Edwards. We've been dealing with him. I'm sure if there was a will it would have come up in conversation. We've been talking about your claim on the estate. I'll have another chat to him, see if he can shed any light. And in the meantime, I gather you're happy to move out of the hotel and give vacant possession to my clients?'

She nodded. She'd forgotten the luxury of proper accommodation, and last night was like a dream. She had no urge to return to the nightmare. 'It wasn't safe.'

'It certainly wasn't. The roof fell in last night,' Nick told them all. 'I've been in there this morning. The mattress is buried under tons of rubble. Dan got you out in the nick of time.'

Beside her Daniel closed his eyes and let out a long, slow breath. 'Hell's teeth,' he muttered. 'Really?'

'Really. We're knocking it down today before anything else can happen.'

She felt sick. Her hands instinctively went to her baby, her fingers stroking it, her eyes fixed on Dan's face. He reached out a hand and touched her shoulder lightly, and she smiled.

Whatever anyone else thought, he'd done the right thing, and they both knew it. Nick, too, for boarding it up so she couldn't get back in there.

The solicitor cleared his throat. 'Right, well, then, I think the next thing to do is to get some information from you about this claim.'

'I'm not sure we need everyone for that,' Dan said, looking at the others pointedly. 'Do we?'

They all shook their heads. 'Do you gentlemen have anything further to add?' the solicitor asked.

'A contract of employment,' Dan said promptly. 'To protect Iona and give her proper employee's rights.'

'OK. I'll do that with her, too, and let you look

it over and have your say when it's done. If that's all?'

'That's all, I think?' Dan said, and the other two nodded. 'We'll go back to the hotel, then, shall we, and carry on there? Iona, would you care to join us when you're finished? It's not far from here. We'll be in the office.'

'OK. Which door?'

'The side door, by the security guard.'

She smiled. 'Tell him to let me in, would you? We aren't best friends.'

Dan's mouth tightened. 'I'll tell him.'

'She's nice.'

Dan rolled his eyes at Harry. 'I said she was nice.'

'Pleasant, well-spoken, educated—'

He sighed, and Harry pulled a face. 'Em was afraid you were getting involved with some little slapper who was after your money.'

'And Brian Dawes's money—and I think the expression was "conniving shark",' he pointed out, and Harry winced.

'Ouch.'

'Indeed.'

'She needs to meet her.'

'Oh, absolutely, but I'm not sure Iona wants to meet her, and I can't say I blame her. I wouldn't. It's a miracle she didn't just walk off and never speak to any of us again.'

'That may be something to do with a lack of options,' Nick pointed out as they turned the corner into the hotel car park. 'But I have to say I agree with you about her, and I think she's sound. She was fantastic when she was working here,' he added. 'A real asset. It would have gone under long before without her, I suspect, because Brian's health was pretty rough. I'd already started negotiating with him before the son came back from Thailand, and he was more than ready to give up. I think he was only hanging on in case either of his sons changed their minds. If I'd realised she was the squatter, I would have talked to her directly and we could have sorted this out ages ago.'

'Well, we know now, and she's out safely, thank God, and maybe we can help her,' Harry said.

'You could start by convincing my sister that she's not a conniving shark,' Dan said drily, and veered off to the security guard's hut. 'Miss Lockwood's going to be joining us. Don't try and stop her, please,' he said, and the man frowned.

'Miss Lockwood?'

'Our sitting tenant. She says you aren't best friends.'

His face went carefully blank. 'Just going my job, Guv.'

Dan grunted and rejoined the others. 'Right, let's get stuck in.'

It was odd coming back.

She walked in through the side door and went through to Reception in the big central foyer. The carpeted hush had been replaced by the crashing and banging upstairs and the sound of the wrecking ball demolishing the annexe on the other side of the car park.

It was familiar, and yet not. The carpets had gone, the fittings were all out except for the re-

ception desk, and it was just a shell, echoing
strangely with the sound of drilling and hammer-
ing, a radio playing cheesy pop and someone
singing along with it out of key.

She closed her eyes and saw it as it had been,
with Brian smiling at her across the scarred old
desk with the brass bell on it, and she felt a now
familiar wave of grief. She squeezed her eyes
tight until she was under control again, then
opened them. The poor old desk. She loved it,
bearing as it did all the marks of the hotel's one
hundred and fifty year history. She thought of all
the people who'd checked in there, the stories
they would have had to tell. And now it was
going to go. She ran her hand over it lovingly,
and it came up covered in fine dust.

Ashes to ashes.

She swallowed and turned away, to find Dan
watching her.

'You OK?' he asked softly, and she nodded.

'I haven't been in here since the funeral. It's all
so different now.'

'Not as different as it will be.'

No. She'd realised that, and had to let it go. 'So what are you planning? Are you going to gut it and make it all modern?'

He laughed. 'Not at all. We'll restore the old hotel, and the rest is being purpose built. We're turning it into a residential spa and health club, so it will still be a hotel of sorts, but there'll be all sorts of fitness and beauty areas, treatment rooms for massage and physio and aromatherapy, that sort of thing—maybe some reiki or shiatsu. And a swimming pool, steam room and sauna. It's a huge site, and it's grossly under-used, and there isn't a health club for miles.'

'Filling a niche?'

'Exactly. Come into the office and meet Georgie's father, George Cauldwell. He's our builder. I'll show you the plans, and then we need to go shopping. How did it go with the solicitor?'

'Fine. He's getting it all under way. Thanks for leaving us to it—and thank you so much for letting me use him,' she added softly. 'I don't know if anything will come of my claim, but at least I'll know I've done all I can for her.'

'My pleasure,' he said, and his smile did funny things to her heart. Either that or it was indigestion.

She'd put her money on his smile.

Nick was on the phone when they went back in, and he was obviously talking to Georgie.

He looked up and smiled at Iona, and Dan wasn't sure if her answering smile was as confident as it appeared. Probably not, but that wouldn't be surprising.

'No, I don't think we'll be much longer. I think we've just about finished here, haven't we, George?'

George gave him the thumbs up, and he nodded and went on, 'Yeah, he says we're done so we'll be out of here soon. Why?'

His gaze flicked to Iona, and he pulled a thoughtful face. 'I don't know. Dan was going to show her the plans and then take her shopping for some clothes, I think. Hers all got ruined.' He paused, and they could hear Georgie talking, protesting. 'About the same as you? OK, well, I'll see you in a minute. I'll tell them to hang on.'

He turned his phone off and looked up at them. 'Georgie's on her way out with the girls. She's going to pop in—she's got some things for you.'

'Me?' Iona said, looking startled.

'Mmm. Maternity clothes. She said it was silly you buying any for such a short time when she's got hundreds and she's about your size. She's going to drop some in.'

Hell. Dan wasn't at all sure how that would go down. She'd flatly refused his offer to ask Emily, but maybe Georgie was different. Apparently so, because when she spoke, Iona was nothing but gracious.

'That would be lovely. Thank you. It would be useful to borrow one or two things just to tide me over until I get my own.'

Borrow—and for the shortest possible time. Reaching out to touch the olive branch? Not that it was Georgie who'd said anything, but if she was wary of all of them, he wouldn't blame her.

Interesting. And it revealed another facet of

a woman he was beginning to find intrigued him more and more...

Ten minutes later, she'd been introduced to George, had seen the plans for the leisure club complex and she had a huge bag of clothes, dropped off by Georgie on her way out with the children. She hadn't come into the hotel, so Iona hadn't gotten to meet her.

Pity. She could have summed her up a little better, but Nick had gone out to get the bag when she'd rung to say she was in the car park, and now she and Daniel were on their way home so she could try them on.

A moment later, alone in her little flat with her emotions, she tipped the whole lot out on to the bed and stared at the clothes in longing. Classy linen trousers, a soft jersey dress, battered jeans, crazy denim bib shorts, T-shirts, a zippy top— the whole shebang, scooped out of storage by Georgie and smelling of fabric softener.

Lovely, after mould and mildew and rotten washing. She pressed her nose into the jersey dress and breathed deeply, and felt herself tearing up again. She put the dress down and lifted the clothes one by one, studying them.

The dress was a beautiful cut, as were the trousers, and the tops looked really useful. There was even a bra. A proper bra, not a flimsy little cotton thing, but a proper, supportive and yet pretty bra with cups the size of melons. It would never fit, she thought, but she tried it on anyway and discovered to her surprise that it did. Not only did it fit, it was comfortable, and pretty, and she felt nearer to sexy in it than she had in ages. And she didn't have four boobs, for a change.

Amazing.

She tried a pair of black linen trousers with a vest top and a loose natural linen shirt, and stared at herself in the mirror. Good grief. She looked almost respectable. No. More than that. She looked as if she could hold her head up in the street again, and after the past few weeks and months, it was enough to bring those wretched tears to her eyes again.

'Don't be stupid,' she muttered, and picked up the jersey dress that she'd buried her nose in.

It was gorgeous. Soft and clingy, and yet elegant. She looked at the label and flinched. It certainly wasn't a chain store cheapy, that was for sure. No wonder it felt so nice.

And looked so good, once it was on.

There were some flat sandals, and as she pulled them out of the bag, a note fluttered out:

Hope some of these are of use. Sorry you've had such a dreadful time the last few weeks. Give me a ring when you've had a look and we can have coffee and sort through the rest of my clothes. Crazy to buy any, I've got tons! Georgie.

She swallowed hard, and sat down on the bed with a bump. A girly coffee. She hadn't done that for ages. So long that she could hardly remember the last time.

There was a tap on the door. 'Iona? Are you OK?'

'Fine,' she said, blinking back the tears, and went to the door, opening it and walking back to the bedroom. 'They're lovely. It was really kind of her. She's invited me for coffee. What do you think? Should I go? And what do you think I should wear? I don't know her, you do. Not this, obviously, it's too dressy. Any ideas?'

She turned back to him and realised he was staring at her as if she'd committed some terrible *faux pas*, and she stepped back, her new confidence starting to crumble into dust. 'Um— maybe I should just stick to my jeans—'

'No! No—you look great. It's lovely. I'm sorry, I just—it took me by surprise. Seeing you like that. You look—'

He broke off, and for an endless moment his eyes burned into her, then he looked hastily away. 'Um—I need to go back to the hotel. Something's come up. If you want a lift to Georgie's, I can take you, but I need to go now-ish. And wear something casual—jeans or whatever. Georgie doesn't do formal when she's got the babies crawling all over her.'

And he backed out of the door as if the room were on fire.

Why?

She turned and looked in the mirror, and then it dawned on her. The dress was a wrapover with a low V, and with the new bra there was more than a hint of cleavage. And she had a waist, even though the bump stuck out. She looked—sexy?

Heavens.

She took the dress off with trembling fingers, tried on the jeans and a pretty top, and felt a little better. Now all she had to do was open the door and go back out there to Daniel and pretend that nothing had happened.

Not that she had the slightest clue what had happened, but it *had* rattled her, whatever it was, and she had no intention of going there again.

Beautiful.

That was what she looked like in the dress. Beautiful, and sexy, and all woman, with her hair down round her shoulders, soft and glossy and making him itch to sift it through his fingers...

He went out into the garden and dragged in a lungful of air. Pebbles was lying on the paving soaking up the sun, and he picked her up carefully and brought her inside.

Iona appeared in the doorway, her hair up again, pulled out of the way into a ponytail and then folded into some kind of loose, messy bun the way Georgie and Emily did theirs. She'd changed into jeans and a pink top that was, if anything, even sexier than the dress, and he swallowed. Her eyes were wary, and he hoped his smile was a little more convincing than it felt.

'Ready?'

She nodded. 'I'd better put the cat in my room,' she said, and took it from him, but their fingers brushed and he felt as if they'd been burned. Iona backed away from him, then turned and walked swiftly back to her room, shutting the cat in and coming back, her front a drift of multi-coloured fur on the pale pink top.

'Um—you've got cat fur,' he said. All over the bump. Damn. And on those breasts. Had they been that size yesterday? Really? He dragged his eyes off them and went into the utility room, coming back with a sticky roller. 'Here.' He handed it to her. There was no way he was running that over her body!

'Better?'

'Fine,' he said, trying not to look too hard and, putting the roller down on the table, he tossed his keys in the air and caught them. 'I've phoned Georgie and she's in. You're going for lunch. Let's go.'

She had a wonderful time.

Georgie greeted her at the door with a welcoming smile and a baby on her hip, and drew her inside.

'Hi, there, it's lovely to meet you,' she said, and looked her up and down. 'Oh, they're a brilliant fit! I'm so glad.'

'They are. Thank you so much. It's just amazing to have something that fits round the bump! I'm really grateful.'

'You're welcome. Iona, this is Lucie. Say hello, Lucie. Come on in; Maya's drawing on the kitchen table,' she said, and took her through to the kitchen. Lucie must have been about nine or ten months, and Maya was probably two, she thought. She looked up from her drawing and gave Iona a great big smile, and within seconds she was admiring the picture and being offered a drink.

'Want juice? Me having juice,' Maya said, sliding down off the chair and heading for the fridge.

Georgie took the carton from her before she dropped it and poured the drinks, then handed one to Iona. 'That top looks lovely on you. Nick said you were about my size, but I didn't really believe him. Men are usually dreadful with things like that. Was anything else any good?'

'Wonderful,' she said honestly. 'Well, I expect so; I didn't have time to look at much. I tried on the black dress—the wrapover?'

'Oh, that one. Nick always adored it. It's really comfy; I wore it loads. I've got a few more things like that, but I wasn't sure what sort of person you were—girly or practical or whatever.'

Girly? She'd never been girly in her life, but she had the sudden urge to try it.

Although from the look on Daniel's face, maybe that wasn't such a good idea.

'Let's go in the garden. I've made us a picnic—shall we go and have lunch, girls?' Georgie said.

Lucie gave her a big grin and said, 'Mum-mum-mum,' happily.

Georgie looked down at her. 'Actually, Iona, could you do me a favour and take her for me, and I'll bring the cool box? Thanks.' And she handed the baby over.

'Hello, sweetheart,' Iona said, smiling at her, and was rewarded with a gummy grin of her own, complete with three tiny little teeth. And she was going to be a mother? Heavens. What an amazing thing to come out of such a dreadful year.

She followed Georgie and Maya out to the garden, winding through the centre of the house, through a big playroom smothered in toys and games, and out of the French windows on to a lawn that overlooked the sea.

It was a fabulous house—nothing like Daniel's but a Victorian Italianate villa with a big square tower, set up above the prom and the beach—and over lunch Georgie told her about

the restoration of the house and the development of the other buildings on the site two
years before.

'Daniel said you were an architect,' Iona said.

'*Were* being the operative word,' Georgie
replied, wrinkling her nose. 'I do the odd bit
now, but with four children it's a bit of a struggle.
I can always go back to it later, and I worked with
Dan on his house. That was fun—a bit of a rush.
Dad built it for him, and because they wanted to
start on the hotel they pushed on a bit and
finished it in six months from breaking ground.
I don't think Dan minded, though. He was so
pleased to get in. You met my father this
morning, incidentally. George Cauldwell.'

'Oh—yes. Nice man.'

'He is, but I'm a bit worried about him. It's a
huge job—not his usual sort of thing, but he's
enjoying the challenge. He had a bypass op two
years ago and he had to take it easy for a while,
but he's right back in the swing of it now. I'm
trying to stop him overdoing it but I'm wasting
my breath. Nick drags him into meetings and

makes him sit down and chat for a while if he thinks it's all getting too much.'

Yes. Iona could imagine Nick doing that; he struck her as a nice man. And Georgie was lovely. Witty and sparky and full of fun, and the girls were delightful and very cuddly.

Once they'd finished eating Georgie put them both down for a nap while they trawled through her maternity clothes.

Iona tried lots of them on, and even though she felt guilty about it, Georgie's comment that it was pointless buying any when hers were going begging did make sense.

'I'll let you have them back as soon as I've finished with them,' she promised as they packed her chosen items into a bag.

'When's the baby due?'

'The beginning of August. About eight weeks. I can't wait to meet her.'

'Her?'

Iona nodded and stroked her tummy affectionately. 'So they said, at the twenty week scan. Hope it's right. I've got used to her being a girl.'

Georgie smiled. 'Girls are lovely. Not that I don't adore the boys, but the girls are special. Well, they all are, of course they are. You'll meet them later, if you're still here. In fact, as the men are tied up all day, do you want to come to the school with me and pick the boys up, and then we can come back here and maybe everyone can come over for supper.'

Everyone? Including Emily?

She didn't feel ready for that—or the yummy mummies at the school gate.

'I really ought to be getting back,' she said with a certain amount of regret. 'After all, I am supposed to be Daniel's housekeeper and if I don't earn my keep—well, I have to,' she said with a wry smile. 'But thank you, anyway.'

'My pleasure.' Georgie handed her the bag of clothes at the door, then hesitated. 'You know, Emily's a lovely person. I know she said some awful things yesterday, but she loves Dan, and she's worried about him. We don't know what Kate did to him, he won't talk about it, but one minute they were like a permanent feature, and the next he was back here from New York and building a house. Anyway, it's none of my business, and he'll tell you if he wants you to know, but she's just worried he'll get hurt all over again.'

'Georgie, I'm his housekeeper,' she pointed out, and Georgie laughed softly.

'Really? Just his housekeeper? We'll see.'

'I am. And that's all. I don't want to be involved with anybody, and it doesn't sound like he does, either.'

But Georgie just smiled. 'We'll see,' she said again, and then, to Iona's surprise, she leant forward and hugged her. 'Take care. Ring me if you need anything.'

'Thanks. And thank you for a lovely day.'

'My pleasure. I'd run you home, but the girls—'

'It's fine; it's a gorgeous day and it isn't far. I'll enjoy the walk.'

And it would give her time to get her thoughts

in order—most particularly the niggling little one that kept wondering what it would be like to be involved with Daniel Hamilton...

CHAPTER SIX

'SO HOW was your day?'

Iona smiled. 'Tiring.'

'That bad, eh?'

'Oh, no, it was lovely,' she said quickly. 'But I am tired. Georgie's gorgeous but she made me try on loads of clothes, and the children are quite full on and I'm not used to it at the moment. And then I went shopping.'

'Oh, lucky you. I loathe shopping, it's my all-time favourite pet hate,' he said with a grin.

'Well, I didn't really have a choice. I had a look through the freezer and it was even emptier than the fridge, so I walked into town and bought some things for supper.'

'You walked? And did *food* shopping?' He sounded shocked, and she laughed.

'Well—yes. I don't have a car. What else did you think I was shopping for?'

'God knows. Women and shopping are a mystery to me. You should have rung me.'

'I don't have a phone.'

'Well, there's one here.'

'But I don't know your mobile number.'

He sighed and rubbed a hand through his hair, leaving it rumpled and sexy. Oh, dear. That again. Then he shot her a thoughtful look. 'Can you drive?'

She stopped looking at his rumpled hair and smiled. 'Well, now—are you asking me if I *can* drive, or if I'm *allowed* to? Because yes, I can, and no, I'm not. I don't have a UK driving licence.'

'Oh. Pity.'

'Why? Got a spare BMW lying around?' she asked lightly, and he chuckled.

'No. But I do have a lovely old TR6 in the garage that comes out from time to time, and I could have used that and lent you the BMW.'

'Not the TR6?'

He shook his head and pulled a wry face. 'Sorry. That's my baby. Not even my father gets to drive that, and he was a policeman.' He glanced towards the kitchen. 'So what did you get? I'll start cooking.'

'You? But it's my job—'

'Not tonight,' he said firmly. 'Tonight I'm doing it.'

'But you cooked last night,' she said, her brow furrowing. 'And it is supposed to be my job.'

'In that case,' he said, 'I'll compromise. I'll let you sit there at the table and tell me what to do. You're a woman—that should be right up your street.'

She laughed and shook her head. 'No. I can't do that. It's not fair.'

'Oh, go on, I'm sure you can bring yourself to do it. Emily tells me what to do all the time.'

And then he let out a sigh, his smile fading as he gave her an apologetic look. 'I'm sorry. I wasn't going to mention her.'

Iona found a smile. 'Dan, she's not going to go

away. I'm going to have to learn to live with her opinion of me.'

'She doesn't have an opinion of you. She has an opinion of a fictional woman she's never met—but that won't last. She's round here all the time. She's a garden designer and she's doing a bit of landscaping for me. You'll probably meet her in the morning—and, if it's any consolation, it'll be harder for her than it will for you.'

She doubted it.

'I'll cope,' she said. 'So—how about penne pasta with crayfish tails in fresh tomato sauce with a touch of chilli and stirred through with cream, and a side salad?'

He blinked. 'You can cook that?'

'No,' she said blithely. 'You can. And if you're very good, I'll tell you how.'

'Oh, I'm very good,' he murmured, and then the air suddenly changed, becoming almost solid, so she could hardly drag it into her lungs.

For a breathless moment they stared at each other, then he seemed to collect himself and turned away, rummaging in the fridge while she fanned her flaming face and told her lungs how to work again.

He'd been flirting with her? Really?

Really.

Even though she was just his housekeeper?

But in her head she could hear Georgie's voice saying, 'Really? Just his housekeeper? We'll see.'

Why on earth had he said that?

He must be nuts. She was pregnant, grieving for Jamie—although why she'd waste emotion on such a useless example of the human race he couldn't imagine, but there was no accounting for taste—and anyway, he wasn't interested in another relationship. Most particularly not one with so many strings attached.

So why on earth was he flirting with her?

Because she was funny and fascinating and liked the same kind of things he did? Because she teased him? Because she was beautiful? She'd been open and friendly when he'd first met her, a little wary, which was natural, but essentially open, and she was beginning, slowly, inch by inch, to open up to him again, and he realised he wanted that, wanted to get to know her, to find out more about her.

He wanted to spend time with her in a way he hadn't wanted to spend time with a woman since—well, for years. Even Kate hadn't made him feel so curious, so keen to get to know her. Not that he ever really had, apparently.

And he didn't know Iona, so if he had a grain of sense he'd back off and stop being so stupid. What if Emily was right?

No. He *knew* she wasn't right, and Emily would, too, the moment she met Iona. But that didn't mean he should get involved with her.

Even if she was the sexiest woman he'd met in years.

He stopped dead, his fingers locked on the fridge door, and he stared into its depths in confusion.

Sexy? Seven months pregnant, and *sexy*? Really?

Oh, God, yes, his body was telling him. Very, very sexy. Not trivially sexy, not superficially, tartily sexy, but deeply, in a sort of earthy, all-woman way that would endure for ever. Even when she'd lost her looks, when she was old and grey and everything was going south, she'd still have that elemental, almost spiritual sensuality that could bring him to his knees.

And it was a damn shame that he wouldn't be there to enjoy it, but he wouldn't. Wrong time, wrong place.

'So,' he said, letting go of the fridge door and straightening up. 'What am I looking for?'

He was a good cook.

He'd led her to believe that he couldn't cook, but in fact he could, and he cooked well. Under instruction, at least, and he confessed he'd never attempted that dish before, but that didn't mean he couldn't do it. And the casserole he'd made last night had been delicious.

Maybe he just didn't like cooking, or maybe he couldn't be bothered just for himself. She could understand that.

Whatever, it was gorgeous, and they sat down together at the dining table, looking out over the sea with their backs to the mess in the kitchen that she knew she'd have to go and clear up in a minute, and they talked.

He talked about how he'd found the plot, about building the house, and his plans for the garden.

'It needs something simple—there was nothing much here to speak of when I bought the plot, no shrubs or trees except for a few old things down each side and a million brambles, and the retaining wall at the end there was broken and crumbling towards the cliff, so the first thing we did was clear the lot and then make it safe. The end's been remodelled so the top of the new retaining wall's level with the lawn, and then it slopes down to a new wall and fence above the cliff. I was going to plant a hedge down there in the autumn, to give a bit more privacy, but as Em said, it isn't really necessary and she's talking about a sedum bank. Apparently they'll love the dry, free-draining conditions. There's a path down to the beach— did you notice that this morning?'

She nodded. 'I tried to go down, but it was locked.'

'Because it's a public beach. I don't want everyone thinking they can use it as a shortcut to the top.'

'No, God forbid.'

He shot her a look. 'Think of the security aspects—and anyway, I value my privacy—is there something wrong with that?'

'No, of course not,' she said with a little smile. 'I'm just not used to things like security and privacy and I've never had anywhere that was my own, so it's just foreign to me.'

'What about when you were at university?'

She shrugged. 'I shared a flat, and had to share a room, so I didn't even have that to myself. Then I was with Jamie, and we were in youth hostels and sleeping on the beach in Thailand and things like that. You don't get much privacy there.'

'No, I can imagine not,' he said, but he looked as if he couldn't imagine it at all, and she thought he'd probably had his own room in a big house when he was growing up, and never had to share anything in his life.

And now he had this, all to himself. Why?

'Why build something so huge?' she asked, echoing her thoughts without stopping to wonder if it was prudent.

Instead of answering he looked out across the sea and his face was sad. 'I don't know. It just seemed right for the plot. I've wanted to build a house like this for years, and I got the chance. And realistically I had to look at resale and maximising its potential, as well, because I won't stay here for ever.'

'Why not?'

He turned to her with a little frown. 'Well—because it's a family home.'

'I know. So why build it? Just for you? Really purely for economic reasons, and as a showcase? That's what you said before, but it doesn't make sense.'

He looked away. 'Does it have to?'

Was that a tic in his jaw?

'No. No, it doesn't have to make sense. Why should it? Nothing else in the world seems to.'

He threw her a smile at that, and went back to the topic of the garden. 'I had the lawn relaid after the ground source heat pump plumbing was put in underground, and now I want to work on some planting at the sides. Nothing distracting, though. I want the sea to be the main focus.'

'I agree,' she said, not letting herself think about that little jumping muscle in his cheek and the defensive look in his eyes before she'd let it drop. 'I don't think you want colour—nothing fussy or cottage garden. Maybe just white flowers, if any at all?'

He nodded, and his smile was wry. 'That's what Emily said. She's drawn a few designs— want to see them?'

'I'd love to.' Even if she was still halfway to hating Emily.

No, she warned herself. Don't judge her, or you'll be just as guilty as her.

The drawings were interesting, but it was his studio itself that fascinated her more than anything.

It was, as he'd warned, chaotically untidy, and there were boxes everywhere. Boxes of books, boxes of paperwork, all sorts of things.

'Excuse the mess,' he said as they went in.

'I've had everything shipped from New York and I need to go through it. I just haven't had time.'

He moved a box off a chair so she could sit down, and as he put it down a photo slid out of the top of it and drifted to a halt at her feet. She bent and picked it up and handed it back to him, and as she did so she saw his jaw clench again.

'Who's Kate?' she asked, guessing, and he threw the photo down and turned away, but not before she'd seen the flash of hurt and disillusionment in his eyes.

'Nobody,' he said, and her heart ached for him, alone in his great big house with nobody to share it, no future in sight, and a girl called Kate with waist-length blonde hair, who'd held his heart in her hands and thrown it away.

What a foolish woman. Had she no idea what she'd had, what she'd lost?

Or what he'd lost because of her?

'So—let's see these drawings, then,' she said, and tried to pretend an interest in something other than the sadness in his eyes and the scent of musk and citrus and soap drifting from his body, and the echoing emptiness of his heart.

The doorbell rang the next morning, just after Dan had gone to the hotel for another site meeting with George Cauldwell.

Iona was getting to grips with her duties, trying to fathom out the central vacuuming system and giving up in favour of mopping the floor, when she heard the sound ring through the hall.

Odd. She'd thought the intercom from the gate would signal visitors, but this was definitely the doorbell, and the only other time she'd heard it had been on Sunday.

And that had been Emily.

So she wasn't altogether surprised when she opened the door and a young woman with long, dark, wavy hair and troubled eyes was standing there. Even though she'd only ever seen her from the back, she recognised her instantly, and the car on the drive was the one she'd seen on Sunday.

Oh, help, she thought. She didn't feel ready for

this, but then she realised she'd never be ready, and it might as well be now as any other time.

For a moment neither of them spoke, but then she straightened her spine and took the bull by the horns.

'Hello, Emily,' she said. 'I'm Iona.'

Emily stared at her for a second, then swallowed. 'Can we be civilised about this, or do you want me to go?'

'Well, it isn't really up to me, is it?' she said softly. 'It's Dan's house, you've come to do the garden—you've got more right to be here than I have.'

'Actually, I've come to talk to you.'

Iona stepped back. 'Well, then, you'd better come in,' she said, and closed the door behind her. 'Coffee?'

'Not yet.'

There was an awkward pause. It was never going to be anything but embarrassing, but Emily frowned slightly, as if she didn't know where to start, and then, meeting Iona's eyes, she said directly, 'I owe you an apology. I shouldn't have said what I did without meeting you, and giving you the benefit of the doubt, but I know my brother and my husband, and they're soft as lights. They wouldn't see a brick wall till they walked into it, and they're very big on the weaker sex thing. Sometimes they just need protecting from themselves, but I'm sorry you heard it. It wasn't meant to be personal.'

Iona grimaced. 'Well, it couldn't be, could it, since you didn't know me,' she said frankly. 'And I understand where you were coming from, but it felt pretty personal at the time, believe me. It wasn't just what you said that upset me, anyway, it was the fact that Daniel hadn't told me he was connected to the hotel and so everything he'd said suddenly seemed like a lie.'

'I can imagine. But he wouldn't lie to you, Iona. He's not like that. He might not tell you everything—in fact he can be infuriatingly obtuse and guarded, but he doesn't lie and he certainly doesn't cheat. And I'm really sorry you were so hurt, but I meant what I said, and I'll say it again to your face,' she went on, her voice quiet but no less forceful for that. 'Don't hurt him. Don't cheat him, don't swindle him or screw him over, or you'll have me to deal with. He doesn't deserve it.'

Well, that was plain enough, Iona thought, and in a way she admired Emily for sticking to her guns.

'Fair enough,' she said. 'But I can assure you I have no intention of screwing him over or taking him to the cleaners. You don't have to fear me.'

'Good. I love my brother to bits, and he's been through hell. I don't want to see it happen again.'

'Kate?' she said, and Emily blinked.

'He's told you about Kate?'

'No. You said something about her on Sunday, and last night in his studio I saw a photo of a woman with long blonde hair.'

'That would be her.'

She nodded. 'I thought it might be. So I asked him who Kate was, and he clammed right up and said, "Nobody."'

Emily gave a grim smile. 'I couldn't have put it better myself, but it's not my story to tell.

You'll have to ask him about her, but don't expect an answer. The rest of us haven't had one yet. And I'm sorry for upsetting you. Can we start again?'

'I think that would be a good idea,' Iona said and, summoning a smile, she held out her hand. 'Hi. I'm Iona.'

Emily smiled back, her eyes soft. 'I'm Emily. It's good to meet you,' she said, and shook her hand.

'So—coffee?'

'I gather you met Emily.'

'Mmm. She's nice.'

He gave a sigh of relief and smiled. 'Funny, she said the same about you. I thought you'd get on.'

'Well, let's not push it,' she said. 'She's left some more drawings in your studio, by the way.'

'Where?'

'I don't know. I haven't been in there. I've been busy.'

'Busy?'

'Oh—you know,' she said breezily. 'This and that.'

This and that? 'Right. Well, I could do with a shower. Something smells nice, by the way.'

'Chilli,' she told him. 'I don't know if you like it, but I've been a bit tied up so I didn't have time for anything elaborate, and you didn't say what time you'd want to eat, so I thought it would keep for another day if necessary.'

'Where did you get the mince? You haven't walked into town again, have you?'

'Emily took me shopping—oh, and she said something about an old bike in the garage at their house. A shopping bike, with a basket or something? It belonged to Harry's grandmother, I think she said. Anyway, she's going to ask Harry if he minds lending it to me so I've got some transport.'

'A bike?'

'Well, yes. What's wrong with that?'

He frowned, horrified at the prospect of her wobbling about on a bike at this stage of her pregnancy. 'Nothing at all, if you've got a death wish. But an old one—has it got lights?'

She laughed. 'Dan, it's the summer! I'm not going out for a bike ride at midnight! I want to be able to get to the shops, that's all. Go on, go and have your shower, I've got to get the washing in.'

'In?'

'Mmm. I got a washing line at the supermarket. You didn't have one.'

'There isn't a post.'

'I know. I tied it to the trees.'

Trees? 'What's wrong with the tumble-drier?'

She rolled her eyes. 'So much for your impressive eco-credentials,' she said, and he frowned again.

'I hate washing on the line.'

'Don't be silly. You can't see it; it's round the side of the house where nobody need ever go. Emily thought it was a good idea. Oh, and I wanted to ask you about having a vegetable patch there.'

He stared at her for a moment, then shook his head in bemusement. 'Whatever,' he said. 'Get Emily to OK it, make sure she doesn't have plans for the area you want to use.' And he headed up the stairs to the sanctuary of his bedroom, wondering what on earth he'd unleashed.

* * *

'Wow.'

'Like it? I used up the fresh chillis from last night.'

'It's good,' he said.

'Too hot?'

'No. It's really tasty. I'm just surprised it's not too hot for you. Emily would choke on it.'

She laughed. 'Dan, I've lived everywhere and eaten everything. Mum and I spent two years in Mexico and Jamie and I were in Thailand for ages. You learn to eat chillis or starve.'

He chuckled and reached for another spoonful from the pot on the side.

'More?' he asked, but she shook her head. Enough was enough, and she didn't want to overdo it. She was running out of room faster these days, what with the baby in the way and everything.

'You OK?'

She realised she was stretching out her side, easing the pressure, and she smiled. 'Just getting a bit crowded in here.'

'I'm sure.' His eyes drifted to her bump, lingering on it like a caress, and then he turned his attention back to the food and cleared his plate. 'That was great. Thanks.'

'Pleasure,' she said, getting to her feet and taking the plate. 'I've made a fruit salad.'

'Ice cream?' he said hopefully.

'I thought you wanted healthy,' she teased, and then got it out of the freezer and waved it at him, and he laughed softly and got up, bringing the rest of the things from the table.

'Witch,' he murmured, reaching past her, and because her bump was getting bigger by the day and she hadn't got used to it, she brushed against him as she turned, and wobbled with the fruit salad in her hands.

'Steady,' he said, his hands on her shoulders, then he let go, taking the bowl from her and putting it down next to the ice cream and leaving her shoulders burning from his touch.

'Why don't you go and sit down and let me do this?' she suggested, suddenly crowded by his big, rangy body in the enclosed space.

'Or I can load the dishwasher while you serve

the fruit salad, and then we can take it out in the garden and sit on the steps at the end and listen to the sea.'

What a silly idea. A silly, romantic, absolutely lovely idea.

They sat there for hours, and when she shivered he went back inside and found her a sweater, a lovely soft cashmere sweater that had a lingering trace of his aftershave on it, and she snuggled into it and sipped the mineral water he'd brought out with him and listened to the sound of the sea, and talked about other beaches she'd sat beside, and Pebbles came and curled up on her lap, and she thought it couldn't get any better than this.

Even if he wasn't hers, even if she didn't really belong here but was just passing through, because that was what she'd always done and nobody had ever said anything about a permanent position.

It was light years from the last few weeks, and she couldn't for the life of her imagine turning back time seventy-two hours, to when he'd found her wrestling with the mattress. It seemed so much more than that. A lifetime ago.

Or certainly a lifestyle.

She had a job, a home, new friends, even if they'd had a bit of a rocky start and things weren't quite comfortable yet. The cat was contented, she was contented and her baby was safe.

'Daniel?'

'Mmm?' His voice was soft, hardly disturbing the night, and she had a crazy urge to lean against him.

'Thank you.'

'What for?'

She smiled in the darkness. 'Being my knight in shining armour. Rescuing me from that awful mess. Taking me and the cat in. Take your pick.'

He chuckled softly. His arm came round her and gave her a brief squeeze, then let go. 'My pleasure,' he murmured, and his voice slid over her nerve-endings and brought them all alive. She could feel the warmth radiating off his body, the heat from his arm around her shoulders, smell the aftershave drifting up from his sweater and from him, and something else, something that did funny things to her insides.

And that probably was indigestion, she thought, and stood up, the cat in her arms. 'I'm going to turn in,' she said.

He got up, too, took her elbow and steadied her on the steps, then walked back to the house with her elbow still cradled in his hand, the glasses clinking in his other hand, and the sound of the surf teasing the shingle beach behind them.

He paused at the door of his studio and, to her surprise, he lifted the hand that had held her elbow and cupped her cheek, his thumb grazing gently over her skin. 'Goodnight, Iona. Sleep well. And thank you for this evening.'

The meal? Or the rest? She wasn't sure, and she wasn't asking. All she could feel was his hand against her cheek, the stroke of his thumb, and she wanted to turn her face into it and press her lips to his palm. But then he dropped his arm and stepped back, freeing her from the spell.

'You're welcome,' she said and, turning on her heel, she took Pebbles through to her little flat, undressed and got into bed and lay there, watching the bright patches on the lawn until the light in his studio went out, and then the hall light, and his bedroom light spilt out into the night.

Then, finally, he turned it off and the night reclaimed the garden. 'Goodnight,' she whispered, and closed her eyes and curled on to her side, her hand tucked under her cheek, where his had touched her so fleetingly.

She could still feel it, she thought, cradling her as she went to sleep...

CHAPTER SEVEN

IONA was a little powerhouse.

Dan came back from the hotel the next evening to find his sheets changed, the towels in his bathroom replaced and the pile of suitcases and clothes in the dressing room next door gone.

And she still had his towelling robe. She seemed to have adopted it, and he wasn't sure he could wear it now without disgracing himself, so he hadn't bothered to get it back. So he had nothing to put on to go in search of her. He contemplated his dirty clothes, and shook his head. No way. They were sweaty and dusty and he'd just got clean. So he wrapped a towel firmly round his hips and ran downstairs.

She was in the kitchen chopping vegetables,

and she looked up and her eyes widened, then shut tight and she swore in a very unladylike way and sucked her finger.

'Grief, Dan, you startled the living daylights out of me!'

'Let me see that.'

He took her hand and straightened out her finger, and the blood welled from the deep, clean slice she'd put in it. 'I don't think it needs stitches—'

'Of course it doesn't need stitches! It just needs a plaster, but I don't suppose you've got any.'

'I have. I have no idea where to find them. There are some in the car, though, but I seem to lack clothes.'

'Ah.' Her finger was back in her mouth, so it was more like 'Argh'. She pulled it out and wrapped it in a paper kitchen towel, squashing it firmly. 'In the cupboards.'

He frowned. 'Cupboards?'

'The great run of wardrobes and stuff down the side of the dressing room? Just where the suit-cases and stuff were? Except for the stuff that's waiting to be ironed. You don't really do

washing, do you? Clothes, that is. You had—
well, must be weeks' worth.'

'It is,' he said, pondering on her impact on his
life and wishing he had the right to kiss her finger
better. No. For heaven's sake, not when he was
only wearing a towel! 'Um—I'll go and find my
clothes. Then I'll get you a plaster.'

And he went back upstairs two at a time,
clutching the towel like grim death and lectur-
ing himself with every stride for his unruly
libido. Inappropriate. Pregnant woman. Grieving
woman. Beautiful, sexy woman—

Damn.

He opened the cupboards and found everything lined up in neat rows. His socks were
paired, his boxers were folded, his shirts were
hung in two banks, short-sleeved and long-
sleeved, grouped by colour—it was amazing.
Like something out of a magazine. He found
jeans, his favourite shirt that had been missing
for weeks, and some very orderly underwear,
threw them on and ran back downstairs and out
of the door to get the plaster.

When he came back in she was in the kitchen with her finger trussed up in tissue and sticking up into the air while she chopped.

'I can do it,' she said, taking the plaster from him and giving him a look when he continued to hover over her. So he went to the fridge and opened it, hunting for a drink while she fiddled with the plaster.

'There's tea in the pot, or I can make you coffee if you don't want a cold drink,' she said.

He shook his head emphatically. 'I've been with builders all day. I never want to see another cup of tea again,' he told her, pulling out a bottle of rosé and unscrewing the cap. 'Want a glass?'

She shook her head. 'Not while I'm pregnant. I'll have fruit juice, though, if you're offering.'

'Sure.' He poured her the juice, handed it to her and peered at the vegetables. 'So what is it tonight?'

'Paella.'

'Rice again.'

She turned, a little frown pleating her brow. He

wanted to straighten out the creases with his thumb. 'Don't you like rice?' she asked.

'I love rice. And pasta. I just wondered if you don't like potatoes?'

'I love potatoes, but they're a bit heavy to carry. Oh, Emily says I can have the bike. Harry's going to do it up a bit and drop it round later. They're coming for supper. She wanted to talk to you about the garden.'

'Right.' So now she was inviting his sister round for supper? 'Thanks for sorting out my clothes, by the way. I didn't even think to look in the cupboard. I just hadn't got round to it.'

'Story of your life, isn't it?' she said mildly, and reached past him for the fridge. 'If you've got everything you need, could you give me a bit of space so I can work?' she asked, and thus dismissed, he picked up his wine and moved out of her way.

'I'll go and make some phone calls, then,' he said, and took himself off. God forbid he should be in her way. In his kitchen.

Oh, don't be petty, he told himself. You just

want to stand next to her and sniff her like a bloody dog. Get over it.

He slid the partition shut and dropped into his chair and stared down the garden.

She was getting to him. Getting to him in all sorts of ways, and if he was going to be able to cope, he was going to have to distance himself from her. No more finding excuses to steady her, or hug her, or touch her unbelievably soft, smooth cheek—

'Oh, stop it!'

He slammed his wine down on the desk, spun the chair and caught sight of the photo of Kate lying on the edge of the desk. Damn. He picked the photo up, held it over the shredder for a second, then put it down again, propped up against his computer, her laughing eyes mocking him. He'd leave it there, to remind him not to make a fool of himself over a woman ever again.

The bike was wonderful, and supper with Harry and Emily was fun.

She didn't overstay her welcome, though, and

the moment they'd finished eating and she'd made everyone coffee and cleared the kitchen, she left them to it. She had things of her own to sort out, clothes to wash and iron, and anyway, eating with them was one thing. Expecting to spend all evening with them was quite another.

So it was ridiculous that she felt so lonely and isolated and cut off in her little flat. Doubly ridiculous since the moment she sat down, Pebbles came and curled up on her lap and went to sleep. She was having a lovely time in the garden these days. She hadn't been upstairs, as far as Iona was aware, but she'd been in his studio, curled up in a filing tray shedding fur for England.

She'd cleared it up, and had to force herself to leave the boxes alone. Especially the one that had had the photo of Kate in it. It was on the corner of his desk, and she'd looked at it.

Hard. That was what her eyes were like, she decided now. Hard and calculating, even though she was smiling. Iona had disliked her on sight, and found it interesting that Emily hadn't liked her, either. She wondered what had happened, but she wasn't going to ask. He'd tell her if he wanted to.

There was a tap on the door, and she shifted the cat and went and opened it.

'Sorry to disturb you,' Dan said, 'but Emily wants to talk about the vegetable patch. She's got hold of this idea and really likes it—wants to do some kind of formal geometric thing, and she wants your advice.'

'Mine?' Iona started to laugh. 'I know nothing about vegetables. I just want to grow them. I've never had a garden before, and I thought it would be fun.'

He frowned slightly. 'Oh. Well—she wants to talk to you, anyway. Why don't you come and join us since you aren't busy?'

'How do you know I'm not?' she asked, and he smiled.

'Because you've got a circle of cat fur on your front,' he said, and walked away, chuckling. She shut the door and followed him.

* * *

It was amazing.

Two days, and Emily, with some help, had transformed the area beyond Iona's end of the house into a gorgeous courtyard garden, with climbers planned to clothe the perimeter walls, and a little vegetable patch and herb garden in the centre surrounded by little gravel paths. There was even going to be room for a bench, set so it faced the sea and would be shaded by a nearby tree from the midday sun. Emily had dug it over, worked in compost and now it was ready to plant.

And, on her new bike, Iona went down to the garden centre next to the supermarket and bought runner beans for the centre of the circle, and French beans and courgettes and lettuces and spring onions to plant around the outsides, and brought them home carefully stacked up in the basket at the front, ready to plant the next day.

She slowed the bike down as she approached the gates, and noticed two women standing looking through them.

'Can I help you?' she said, getting off the bike

and walking up to them, and they turned and smiled a little guiltily.

'Oh, no. We were just looking,' the older lady said. 'I used to live here with my husband, but after he died I couldn't look after it any more and in the end I had to give up. It was just too expensive, and then with the fire...I was just wondering what it had been replaced with, but it's none of my business. I have to let go, but after seventy-five years that's easier said than done,' she added with a little laugh.

But there was a look of longing on her face, and Iona, ever given to impulse, said, 'Would you like to see it?'

'Oh, no, we couldn't trouble you, could we, Mum?' her younger companion said, but her mother was still looking through the gates, and the longing on her face tore at Iona.

'It's no trouble,' she said firmly and, keying in the combination, she pressed the button to open the gates and ushered them through.

'So—do you live here?' the daughter asked.

'Yes—well, sort of. I'm the housekeeper. But

he won't mind,' she said confidently, and crossed her fingers behind her back…

Daniel was exhausted.

He'd been working all day at the site, running up and down stairs, backwards and forwards, checking details and making on-the-hoof decisions as the tradesmen had come to him in turn with one problem after another. And in between he'd been looking for the will without success.

He wanted a shower, clean clothes and a glass of nicely chilled wine in the garden.

What he didn't want was to come into his house—*his* house!—and find Iona sitting there with two strange women having a damned tea party at his dining room table! He stopped dead in the doorway, and she looked up at him with a pleading look in her eyes and said, 'Ah, Daniel, you're just in time. Grab yourself a cup and a plate and come and join us. This is Mrs Jessop. She used to live here. Her husband built the original house. And this is her daughter, Mrs Gray.'

He took a slow, steadying breath and walked towards them, his eyes skewering Iona with a look that should have had her running for cover. But she held her ground, and his eyes, and finally he looked away, dredged up his manners and smiled at the older of the two women.

'Mrs Jessop. It's good to meet you.' And he reached out his hand and took her frail, gnarled fingers in his, and met the rheumy old eyes that had seen too much and lost it all, and his anger faded.

'I do hope you don't mind us imposing like this,' Mrs Jessop was saying, hanging on to his hand. 'We didn't want to put you out, but Iona assured us you wouldn't mind, and it's been so wonderful to see it. I asked my daughter Joan to bring me here, just so I could look down the drive, but I never expected that we would be invited in.'

He hadn't either, but he was suddenly ridiculously glad that Iona had made them so welcome.

He pulled out a chair and sat down, still holding her hand. 'I don't mind at all. I'm delighted to get a chance to talk to you. I didn't

realise your husband had built the original house
or I would have spoken to you earlier.'

'Oh, yes. He built it for us, just after we
married in nineteen thirty-four.'

'Nineteen thirty-four? But that's—what, three-
quarters of a century ago!'

'Which probably explains why I feel ninety-
six,' she said with a smile.

He stared at her. 'Good grief. Well, I hope I
look as good as you when I'm three times my
age,' he said with a grin, and she laughed and
patted his hand.

'Flattery isn't obligatory, you know.'

'Oh, but I believe in giving credit where it's
due,' he replied, and she gave a cracked laugh
and sat back.

'I like you, young man, and I like your house. My
husband would have been delighted to see it. We
didn't have the money to build anything this grand,
but he would have loved to have done. And you still
have the big lawn. Nobody could understand why
we didn't plant anything in the middle of it, but
why would you need to, with that to look at?'

'Absolutely. I quite agree.' He turned to her daughter and gave her an apologetic smile. 'I'm sorry, I'm ignoring you. I'm Daniel,' he said, and shook her hand. 'So—you must have lots of childhood memories.'

'Oh, yes. Lots of fun on the beach—we had a proper beach in those days, but the coast's changing all the time. We had a look down the garden, and the sea's closer now than it used to be.'

'Oh, it is, but it was lovely to see it again. It's years since I could walk to the end of the garden. Not since Tom died in nineteen ninety. It got so overgrown then without him cutting the grass, and I couldn't afford a gardener.'

'It must have been hard living here all that time without him,' Iona said gently.

'It was. Too long—and I let him down. I didn't look after it, but you've done his vision proud, Daniel. He would have loved it.'

He smiled, a little embarrassed by all the emotion just under the surface, but soft enough to be pleased. 'Thank you. That's the nicest thing anybody's said about it.'

'It's only the truth. You've made a lovely home. You're a nice man, Daniel Hamilton. A good man. There should be more architects like you.'

He realised Iona was watching him, a cup in her hand—one of the espresso cups and saucers, the nearest thing he had to a teaset—and notwithstanding what he'd said the other day about tea and the building site, he took it without a murmur, smiled reassuringly at her and accepted a slice of cake to boot.

His teeth sank into it, and he stopped in surprise and shot Iona a look.

'Carrot cake. It's healthy,' she said, and a smile flickered on her lips and was gone.

He chewed and swallowed, and let his own smile out. 'It's very nice,' he admitted. 'Thank you.'

'Pleasure. I made it for Emily—we were doing the courtyard.'

'Courtyard?'

'You know, the pretty little courtyard garden at the end, by Iona's flat,' Mrs Jessop said, beaming. 'It's where Tom always had his vegetable patch, and it'll grow the most wonderful beans. Iona's going to plant them tomorrow. And the water feature will be lovely.'

'Right.'

Water feature? Well, he'd known the vegetable patch was coming, but a courtyard? With a water feature? And beans? Together? That'd teach him not to pay attention to his garden designer and his conniving housekeeper. He had another bite of the gorgeously moist and tasty carrot cake and hid his smile.

'I've got lots of photos of the house when it was being built,' Joan was saying. 'I was going through them with my grandchildren when it burned down, so they were saved. In fact lots of things were saved.'

'But not the house.'

Mrs Jessop shook her head. 'It doesn't matter. I couldn't stay here alone any more, and it needed so much work. It had served its purpose and, if I'm honest, I'm quite glad it's gone. It was so much *our* house. It wouldn't have seemed right to have somebody else living in it. There was too much of Tom in it somehow.'

He could understand that. There was so much of him in this house that the idea of selling it in the future was untenable. Was that why he'd built such a big house? Iona had asked him the other day, and he hadn't really told her the truth, maybe because he didn't know the answer. But was it because he was secretly hoping that some time in the future he'd bring a bride home, a woman who'd give him children—children who'd bring it to life?

A woman like Iona?

He swallowed, and Mrs Jessop reached out and patted his hand. 'You'll get there,' she said softly, as if she could read his mind, and he met her tired old eyes and found a smile.

'We'll see. Has Iona shown you right round?'

'Oh, no. That would be too much. She showed us her flat and in here, and we've walked down the garden. I wouldn't let her show us any more.'

'Fancy a guided tour?'

'I'd love one, but I can't manage the stairs now.'

He eyed her. She couldn't weigh more than Iona's cat. 'What if I carry you?'

She gave a little crack of laughter. 'Heavens. It's years since a man last carried me up the stairs.'

'So, Mrs Jessop,' he asked, winking at her, 'do you want to come up and see my etchings?'

She laughed out loud and patted his cheek. 'Do you know, young man, I believe I might.'

'I'm really sorry.'

'Don't be. She was delightful. They both were, and it wasn't hard, was it?'

'But they're going to come back with the pictures,' she said, washed with guilt. 'It could go on for ever.'

'Hardly,' he said realistically, and Iona nodded.

'No. You're right.' She tipped her head on one side and smiled at him. 'She was right. You are a nice man, Daniel Hamilton. Kind.'

'And dirty,' he said. 'I'm going for a shower, and then I want a drink of something that isn't tea, and food.'

She touched her forelock and grinned. 'Coming right up,' she said, and went back to the kitchen and cleared away the debris of her impromptu tea party, then put the salmon steaks and new potatoes on to cook, dressed the rocket salad and laid the table again.

Poor Daniel. But he'd been a star, just as she'd known he would be once he'd met them, and really risen to the occasion. She couldn't believe he'd carried Mrs Jessop upstairs, twinkling away at her and flirting right, left and centre. The old charmer.

She grinned and went back into the kitchen to check the salmon, humming softly under her breath, and then as she turned she saw him standing there watching her, an enigmatic look on his face.

'So—what's all this about a water feature?' he asked.

They planted the vegetables after they'd eaten, even though he was wearing clean clothes, because, as he said, she could hardly struggle around and plant things when she was seven months pregnant, and he knew perfectly well she'd give it her best shot if he didn't do it first.

And he had to admit it was going to look nice.

'So where's this water feature going?' he asked, and she pointed to the wall behind him. 'There. Well, that's what Georgie said. My kitchen's there, so the power and plumbing won't be a problem, she said.'

'Did she.'

'Yes.'

'So what kind of water feature is this, that I'm no doubt paying for?' he asked, and she blinked and shrugged.

'Search me. Georgie said you ought to choose it.'

'Big of her,' he said drily.

She chewed her lip. 'Don't blame her. It was my idea. Running water is very soothing.'

'It always makes me want to pee.'

She chuckled. 'Well, that, too, but it is restful. We thought this would make a lovely sheltered area for quiet contemplation. Productive, restful—a good place to come when things all get too much.'

'They're all too much now, and I can't say it's helping,' he grumbled, but his heart wasn't in it and he helped her water the little plants in and then stood back and admired them. 'Right. I want another glass of wine, I've got some phone calls to make and then I'm going to crash. What about you?'

'Actually, I'm tired,' she confessed. Well, he'd known that. That was why he was making himself scarce, so she felt able to retreat to her flat and have an early night.

He left her at the door, went into his studio and stared at Kate. She wouldn't have understood him showing Mrs Jessop round at all. Or the beans and lettuces and things, and she would have tossed the water feature off the cliff. Mrs Jessop too, probably.

He put the photo in the shredder, and felt instantly better.

She was more than tired, she was exhausted.

It had been a really long day, what with helping Emily to do the courtyard garden and making the cake, as well as ironing a load of Dan's shirts and trousers, which she'd washed and dried. And then there had been the trip to town to buy the plants, and Mrs Jessop and her daughter, and then planting the seedlings after supper.

And now she was just ready to fall into bed, but instead of winding round her legs and nagging her for food and a cuddle, Pebbles was missing. And her food dish was still sitting there with food in it, and the litter tray hadn't been used. Not that that was surprising, now she could get outside, but everything together made a picture that worried Iona.

A lot.

She searched the flat, looked around outside in the dusk, and then went through to Daniel and tapped on his studio door.

It slid open. 'Hi. What's the problem?'

'I can't find the cat. I wondered if she was in here with you.'

He shook his head, a frown creasing his brow. 'When did you last see her?'

'I don't know. Earlier. She was in the garden with me and Emily this morning. I haven't seen her since then.'

'Did you leave the side gate open when the front gates were open, too?'

She shook her head. 'No. The big gates were closed.'

'But she might have gone into the front garden and be stuck there, now the side gate's shut. Let's go and look.'

They searched the house together, then he turned on the floodlights and they went out into the garden and looked around, checking under bushes and behind bins and anywhere she might have gone.

And then she looked up and he was standing there, looking down at her, and she knew. She pressed her hand to her chest.

'Where is she?'

'Under the old lilac,' he said softly. 'She lay there a lot, in the sun. I've noticed her, because I can see it from my studio. She loved it there in the evening.'

She got slowly to her feet, dragged down by the weight of yet another loss. 'Show me,' she said, her voice rusty, and he took her arm and led her over to the lilac, and there underneath it, curled up as if asleep, was her moth-eaten little cat.

She knelt down and stroked her, but she was cold, the life gone out of her.

'Oh, God, Daniel, I can't do this again,' she said, and a great sob rose in her throat and she covered her mouth to hold it in, but it wouldn't stay there, and it was followed by another, and then another, and he knelt down beside her and rocked her gently in his arms as she cried.

Finally she hiccupped to a halt, and he sat back and looked at her, his eyes concerned. 'Are you OK?'

She nodded. 'It was just—I don't know. She's the only pet I've ever had, and Brian was the only father I've ever had, and I've never really grieved for him, and my baby will never know her father, and it's all just too much—'

The tears fell again, and he gathered her up against his chest and held her there as she cried for Jamie, and for Brian, and for the poor, deaf, scruffy little cat who'd loved her unreservedly.

'I'm so sorry,' he said at last, and she scrubbed away the tears and reached for a tissue, but she didn't have one, and he handed her one from his pocket, all neatly folded, and she wondered if he'd picked it up because he'd known what they'd find under the bushes.

'Can we bury her here?' she asked, and he nodded.

'Of course. I'll get a spade.'

He disappeared, and came back a minute later with a shoe box full of tissue paper and the spade, and while she watched he gently lifted the cat into the box, covered her with the tissue and put the lid on, then started digging.

It didn't take long and, when it was done, she stood up awkwardly and stared down at the bare little patch of earth under the bush.

'Are you OK?' he asked softly, and she nodded.

She was. Terribly tired, terribly sad, but she'd felt worse and probably would again.

'I'm OK,' she said.

He drew her into his arms and hugged her gently, then, lifting his head, he stared down at her for a long moment before brushing her lips with his.

As kisses went it was tame, hardly more than the touch of a feather, but it reached right down inside Iona and warmed the parts of her that she'd thought would be cold for ever.

Then all too soon he lifted his head and looked down into her eyes and sighed.

'Come on,' he said gruffly. 'You're exhausted, and you're much too tired to deal with this. Let's get you back inside and make you a drink and get you into bed.'

He wanted to get her into bed? Tired and tear-streaked and seven months pregnant? She gave a slightly hysterical little giggle, and he laughed softly. 'Come on, I didn't mean that,' he said, and she felt a huge wave of regret.

'Sit there and don't move,' he said, depositing her in her sitting room and putting the kettle on, then he disappeared, and she realised he was in her kitchen still, clearing away all the cat's little bits and pieces, and she felt her eyes welling up with tears again.

Oh, it was ridiculous! She'd been ancient, she'd had a lovely peaceful death—it was silly to cry for her, but cry she did, and when Daniel came back into the room he sighed and dropped down on to his haunches in front of her and wiped her eyes.

'Come on,' he said and, drawing her to her feet, he led her through to her bedroom and pushed her gently towards the bathroom door. 'Get ready for bed. I'll be back in a minute with a hot drink.'

And he left her there, standing staring in the mirror at this red-eyed, lost little waif with eyes as old as time, and because she couldn't bear to look into them she cleaned her teeth with her eyes shut, then went to the loo and changed into a lovely nightshirt that Georgie had lent her, and when she walked back out into the bedroom Daniel was sitting there on the bed, a thoughtful look on his face.

'You OK?'

'Do I look OK?' she asked, and he shook his head.

She pulled back the quilt and climbed in, then straightened the covers with meticulous attention before finally looking up and meeting his eyes. 'Stay with me,' she said softly. 'I know I look like Methuselah's mother at the moment and I'm probably the last person in the world you want to be with, but I don't think I can be alone tonight.'

'Oh, Iona.' His sigh was gentle, his hand against her cheek tender. 'You don't look like Methuselah's mother. You don't look old enough to be anybody's mother, and, for what it's worth, I think you're beautiful, but you don't need this tonight.'

God, the rejection hurt. She met his eyes and tried to smile. 'It's OK. You don't have to be kind. Go to bed, Daniel. I'll be fine. And thanks—you know, for the cat and everything.'

For some reason he didn't move. 'I'm not being kind,' he said gruffly. 'I'm trying to be fair to you. I'm not what you want, Iona. I'm damaged goods. Bad news. And your judgement's right off at the moment—'

'Have I asked you for eternity?' she said, and for a moment she thought he'd go anyway, but then he gave a ragged sigh, stood up and peeled off his jeans and T-shirt. He was barefoot, as usual, and he left his boxers on—to protect himself, or her? She didn't care. Then he flipped off the light, slid into the bed beside her and drew her down into his arms.

'Sleep now,' he said. 'We'll talk later.'

Sleep? Was he crazy?

But the warmth of his body and the steady, even rhythm of his heart soothed her, and with his arms close around her, she drifted peacefully to sleep, feeling safer than she'd ever felt…

CHAPTER EIGHT

SOMETHING woke him.

He didn't know what—a noise? It took him a moment to work out where he was, another moment to work out that he was alone.

And there was the noise again. A sob, muffled by distance and the wind, but triggering his protective instinct even in his sleep. He threw back the covers and went through to her sitting room, and found the door open into the moonlit garden.

Iona was kneeling by the lilac, arms wrapped round her body, rocking as she sobbed, and the sight unravelled him.

It was so unfair. How much more could she be expected to take? He didn't know whether to go to her or not. Not, he thought. She'd waited until she could be alone. He had to respect that.

Dan watched as she stood up awkwardly and walked to the end of the garden, sitting down on the steps overlooking the sea. But then she looked so forlorn, sitting there alone staring out over the sea, that he couldn't bear it any more. He went to her, barefoot in the damp grass, and sat down beside her. At first she said nothing, then with a sigh she turned to him and smiled sadly.

'I'm sorry,' she said softly. 'I know I'm being pathetic, but I've just had a basinful recently, and the cat was the last straw. She was just such a sweetie, and I'm going to miss her.'

'Of course you are—and you aren't being pathetic at all. I think you've been incredibly brave about all of it.' He slipped his arm round her shoulders and pulled her against his side, and with a sigh she leant against him and rested her head on his shoulder, propped in the crook of his neck, her hair tickling his ear.

He brushed it back, threading his fingers through it and lifting it away from her face, loving the feel of it. So soft, like silk. Beautiful. She raised her head and looked up at him in the moonlight, and then suddenly everything seemed to shift and change, as if even the sea was holding its breath.

He felt her slim, cool hand settled against his jaw, and he turned his face into it, pressing his lips to her palm. Then he lifted his head and stared down into her eyes.

'Iona?'

He'd spoken so softly he wasn't sure she'd heard him. For an endless moment she did nothing, then he felt her fingers thread through his hair and draw him down, and as he bent his head he felt the warm sigh of her breath whisper over his mouth, just before his lips touched hers.

Then the world settled back on its axis, and the sea breathed again, and everything just seemed right.

'Oh, Iona,' he murmured and, cradling her head in his hands, he kissed her again, and again, until suddenly instead of tenderness there was fire raging through them.

He stood up and pulled her gently to her feet and led her back to her room, leaving the doors open so they could hear the sighing of the sea in the shingle. Then he turned her in his arms and kissed her gently, cupping her shoulders in his hands and staring down into her face. Her expression was hard to read in the dim light, but when she came up on tiptoe and kissed him back, he didn't need to see her.

He let his hands slip down her arms until their fingers linked. 'Are you sure?' he asked, just to be absolutely certain, and she nodded.

'Quite sure.'

'You'll have to tell me what to do. I've never made love to a pregnant woman before.'

She laughed softly. 'I'll tell you when I've worked it out. Do you want to phone a friend?'

He chuckled. 'I'm sure we'll manage.' He slipped his hands free and took hold of the nightdress, gathering it in his fingers until it was bunched up and he could lift it over her head.

She raised her arms for him, and then slowly let them fall as he watched her, spellbound, breathless. All that woman. Dear God. He dropped the nightdress, reached out a hand and stroked it gently over the smooth, taut curve of her child.

'You're beautiful,' he said gruffly. 'I'm so afraid I'll hurt you.'

'You won't hurt me. It's supposed to be good for you.'

'Really?' He smiled at that. 'Like vitamins and stuff?'

He could see her mouth tipping up at the corners. 'Something like that.' He felt her thumbs in the top of his shorts, easing them down, and he kicked them away and let her look at him.

'Wow,' she said softly, reaching out a hand and running her knuckles down over his ribs before turning it and laying her palm flat against his heart. 'I don't suppose I can tell you you're beautiful, can I?'

He gave a surprised laugh and drew her into his arms, then gasped at the feel of her, warm and firm and all woman against him. Heat raced through him and, with a ragged sigh, his mouth found hers and clung.

* * *

She felt amazing.

She'd never felt so loved, so cherished or wanted or beautiful in her life—which was ridiculous, considering she was like a beached whale now. But she didn't feel like one in his arms—she felt glorious. She shifted so she could see him better, lying sprawled beside her with one arm flung up over his head and a knee bent up towards her.

His body was gorgeous. Firm and fit and toned, with just a scattering of hair over his chest that arrowed down to that impressive—

'Do you always watch people when they're sleeping?'

She gave an embarrassed laugh and pulled the quilt up over them both. 'I'm usually alone,' she pointed out, and he rolled towards her and slid a hand round the back of her neck, drawing her closer so he could kiss her.

'Me, too,' he said. 'Well, for a while, anyway.'

She reached up a hand and rested it against his chest, loving the feel of his heart beating just the other side of his ribs, its rhythm steady against her palm. 'Tell me about Kate,' she said, holding her breath, and he went still.

'There's nothing to tell. I don't want to think about her.'

'But you just did. When you said you'd been alone for a while—she came into your thoughts.'

'You're going to nag until I tell you, aren't you?' he said.

'Probably,' she admitted, softening it with a gentle touch to his cheek.

He gave a heavy sigh and rolled on to his back again, tucking her up against his side. 'We were lovers. We worked together for three years on various projects, and for eighteen months she was sleeping with another member of the team.'

She jacked herself up on her elbow and stared down at him. 'Oh, my God—and you were working with them both? Didn't you want to kill him?'

'Her.'

She stared. 'Her?'

'Her. Angie. And how can you compete with that? If it's another man, you're on a level playing field. You have a bigger car, a bigger income, a bigger—whatever. But a woman? Where do you start?'

'So where did you start?' she asked softly.

'I walked away. I sold up, moved out, came back here.'

'And you didn't tell anyone.'

'How do you know that?'

'Because I've asked them about Kate, and they didn't know anything. Emily said it was your story to tell, and good luck to me, because nobody else could get it out of you.'

She rested her head down again and snuggled closer, her hand round his side holding him tight. 'That's so unkind. To sleep with you both, not to tell you, to just—to *lie* to you like that, in that way, for *years*. Horrible. No wonder you ran away.'

'I didn't run. I walked. And she tried to follow me, and I told her to go to hell. And her girlfriend dumped her.'

She tried to feel pity, but couldn't. 'Why didn't

she just say what she felt? Why did she keep up the pretence?'

He shrugged. 'Her father was a church minister. Living with me was bad enough. Living with a woman would have been the end. She couldn't tell them. And I guess the cover suited her.'

'So she used you as cover?'

'Sort of, I suppose.'

She stroked his chest, loving the feel of it, the warmth and strength and beauty of him. How could Kate have done that to him? 'That's a real bummer.'

'Yeah. Whatever, it's over now.'

Was it? She didn't think so. He'd called himself damaged goods. You wouldn't do that if you didn't believe it. And he must have loved her at first.

Mustn't he?

They went shopping for baby things the next day, because it was the weekend and he didn't have to go to work. She told him it was too early to think about baby stuff at seven months, but he was insistent.

'You never know how early it might be,' he said

and, because it made sense, they went—just to look. Only they didn't just look, they bought.

All sorts. A big proper pram, because she'd always wanted one, so she could walk to the shops and put her shopping underneath, and a cot for the bedroom, and a clever carrycot-cum-pushchair-cum-baby-seat like Emily's daughter Kizzy's, and clothes. Not for the baby, because Georgie and Emily had lots of tiny clothes to lend her, but underwear for her. Bras, like the one Georgie had lent her, and some new knickers. Something pretty for Daniel to take off her, she thought, and blushed hotly.

'If you're thinking what I'm thinking, we could well be arrested,' he murmured in her ear, and she blushed even hotter.

'Stop it,' she hissed, and then got the giggles, and they ended up having to leave before they disgraced themselves.

They went to another shop and tried again, and she emerged victorious with a lovely little string-handled bag with a sticky seal on it and lots of gorgeous underwear wrapped in tissue inside it.

She'd protested vigorously about the price, but he'd just grinned wickedly and said it was for him, not for her, and she'd teased him about looking silly in it.

It was a fabulous day. They had lunch out—fish and chips in paper up the coast at Aldeburgh, from an award-winning chip shop, and went for a stroll along the beach and looked at Maggi Hambling's huge and controversial sculpture of scallop shells.

'I love it,' she said, stroking the warm metal thoughtfully.

'So do I. Lots of people hate it—or hate where it's sited. They say it changes the long view down the beach, but I think it's thought provoking and I love the lines of it. Fluid. Beautiful.'

They walked on, beside the marshes, and then they strolled back to the car and drove home again.

Home. Funny, how readily the word tripped off the tongue, she thought. The baby stuff wouldn't be delivered till the following week, but he handed her the bag of underwear with a glint in his eye as they got out of the car, and they got thoroughly sidetracked after that.

He took her out for dinner that night, to the Chinese restaurant where they'd bought the take-away on that first night just a week ago, and afterwards they sat on their bench and held hands and she was stunned to realise that it had only been one week.

It felt like for ever.

He invited the gang round for a barbecue the next day, and then had to rush out and buy one and screw it all together before they arrived. And she had to shop and cook for them, however many there were.

Lots.

She tried to do a head count and got lost, because the children were running about all over the place like ants. Emily and Harry, of course, and Nick and Georgie, and all of their children, to start with. They were joined by George Cauldwell, Georgie's father, who lived a few streets away, and Nick's mother, Liz, who lived in her own flat behind Nick and Georgie's house, where she had her own art studio. And Juliette and Andrew Hamilton, Daniel and Emily's parents, who she'd never met before. Ten adults, then, and seven children ranging from nine years to nine months, and because she felt a little self-conscious of her role—Dan's housekeeper, as well as, very newly, his lover—and not really a bona fide member of the group, she ended up in the kitchen with the food while the grandmothers supervised the children and the men organised the wine and watched the barbecue and Emily showed Georgie the courtyard.

Her courtyard, she thought, but it wasn't, it was his, and it wasn't her fault they didn't realise Daniel was sleeping with her.

It seemed bizarre that only a week before she'd been huddling in a doorway in a thunderstorm, and now the sun had come out and everything had changed. Except, perhaps, it hadn't. She'd been feeling as if she really belonged with him, but now here she was in the kitchen, with a house and garden full of people and feeling, if anything, even more alone.

Not that Georgie and Emily were anything but

nice, but they didn't know things were different now with Daniel, and she wasn't actually sure how different they were. It was more that she felt she didn't belong, and so she was holding herself back.

Then Emily and Georgie came into the kitchen and started helping without being asked, and Georgie was really enthusiastic about her little vegetable garden, and she wondered if she was being silly.

Probably, because when they were out in the garden again and they'd all finished eating, Harry dropped down next to her chair on the grass with a grin and said, 'I gather you've done a lot of travelling. Tell me where you've been.'

And finally she was on safe ground.

She talked about Peru, and Africa, about Papua New Guinea and Borneo, and he told her about Iraq and Kosovo and Indonesia. She discovered he could speak fluent Malay, to her delight, and she tried to practise on him. Hers was a little rusty, but it was fun to try—until she looked up and found Emily watching her thoughtfully.

Oh, hell, she thought, I hope she doesn't think

I'm after her husband! If only Dan would come over and give her a hug, give them all some signals, but Dan seemed to be avoiding her, and only Liz was in range, so she turned to her and asked her about her painting.

'Oh, I just dabble,' she said dismissively, and Harry snorted.

'You're such a liar,' he said benignly. 'Iona, you've seen her work. The seascape in the hall? The triptych in the sitting room?'

'Yours?' Iona said, awed. 'Wow. I wish I dabbled in something like that!'

'I would say you dabble in languages,' Harry said in Urdu, and she smiled and told him, in Swahili, that he was a show-off, and he threw back his head and laughed.

'What on earth are you two on about?' Emily said, bemused.

Oops. Don't upset the enemy, Iona thought, still not convinced that Emily had totally accepted her, but Harry just grinned at his wife.

'She's a natural linguist,' he said. 'And rather too fluent. She just called me a show-off.'

'Comes from having such a random childhood,' she explained. 'Either I learned the lingo or I didn't speak to anyone. It was a no-brainer, really.'

'Well, you're light years ahead of me; I struggled with schoolgirl French,' Emily admitted with a smile. 'Anyone for tea?'

'I'll make it,' she said, moving to get up, but Emily pushed her back down.

'Absolutely not. You sit there and talk international politics and stuff like that with Harry, because you understand it better than I do, and Mum and I'll make the tea, won't we, Mum?'

So Mrs Hamilton followed her daughter with a laughing shrug, and Iona turned back to Harry and said, 'International politics? Really?'

He laughed. 'What would you rather talk about?'

And because she'd never learned to put a leash on her tongue, she said quietly, 'Who was Carmen?'

She regretted it immediately because a shadow went over his face, but he gave a soft sigh and stared out over the sea, plucking a blade of grass and shredding it thoughtfully. 'My first wife.

Well, technically. I married her to save her from an untenable situation, and she died after a stupid accident. She was pregnant, and I ended up with Kizzy. That was when I met Emily again. I hadn't seen her for years.'

'But you've loved her for a long time.'

He shot her a keen look. 'Yes, I have. Did she tell you that?'

She shook her head. 'No. But you've got that sort of confidence in your relationship that comes with knowing each other for years. I envy you that. I've never had that with anyone.'

'Goes with being a nomad, I suppose,' he said, and then tipped his head on one side. 'But I dare say you could settle down?'

She could feel that her smile was unsteady. 'If I was ever in the right place at the right time.'

'And is this it?'

She looked away. 'I don't know. It might be— for me, anyway. I don't know about Daniel.'

'I don't know what happened with Kate, but it hurt him very deeply. Be gentle with him, Iona. He's a good guy.'

'I know that.'

Dan was coming towards them, and Harry smiled and got to his feet. 'I'll go and chase up that tea,' he said, and left her alone with him.

'You OK?' he said, pausing beside her and studying her thoughtfully.

'I'm fine.'

'You sure? You look a little uncertain about that. Are you tired? You can go and lie down if you want. You don't have to stay here with this lot if you've had enough.'

Was that a hint that he wanted her to go?

'No,' he said, hunkering down in front of her and taking her hands. 'That wasn't a hint. I was trying to look after you.'

Could he really read her mind? 'Making sure I get plenty of rest for tonight?' she said, not entirely joking, but his mouth kicked up in a grin.

'Now there's a thought—yours, not mine, but an interesting one.' He stood up, his fingers trailing over her shoulder. 'You've caught the sun. I'll get you some sun cream.'

But it was Georgie who put it on her shoulders, and Harry who brought her the tea, and Emily who came and sat next to her and took her hand and said, 'I'm so sorry about the cat. I didn't know—Daniel's just told me. You should have said. I thought you looked sad.'

And she hugged her, and Iona closed her eyes and hugged her back.

Would this woman who'd been so wary of her a week ago really turn into a lifelong friend? That would be so nice. If only she could dare to believe in it. In all of it, all of them.

Dan caught her eye across the lawn and winked, and she felt something warm and wonderful bubble up inside.

It felt too good to be true, but maybe it wasn't? Maybe it was her turn to find some happiness.

Then George Cauldwell stood up and called everyone's attention. 'I've got something I want to say to you all. Well, firstly to Nick, because I feel I ought to do this properly.' He grinned, and Nick gave him a puzzled look.

'I've asked Elizabeth to do me the honour of

becoming my wife, and she's agreed, so with your blessing, Nick, we'd like to get married.'

Nick's mouth opened, but no words came—just a strangled laugh, and a huge hug for his mother and his father-in-law. 'Oh, you dark horse!' he said at last, sweeping his mother off her feet and whirling her round with a laugh. 'Absolutely.' And he pumped George's hand, and slapped his back, and Georgie was sucked into it, and just when Iona was feeling that it couldn't get any better, Dan came up behind her and bent over, sliding his arms round her shoulders and folding them under her chin, and his lips brushed her temple.

'Well, isn't that lovely?' he murmured. 'I thought they'd never get round to it. I wonder if David'll come home for the wedding.'

'David?'

'Georgie's brother. He's in Australia. He hit me, too, when I kissed her.'

'No wonder you never tried again,' she said with a smile, and he chuckled and hugged her, then straightened up, leaving his hands on her shoulders.

And Harry, glancing across and catching her eye, raised an eyebrow almost imperceptibly and smiled.

CHAPTER NINE

THAT weekend set the scene for the next few weeks.

During the day Daniel either worked at home in his studio, or went down to the hotel, and Iona pottered round the house and cooked their evening meal and kept the laundry under control, and when she had time she'd take a cup of tea outside and sit on the bench he'd had installed in her vegetable garden and watch the beans rushing up the bamboo canes, and turn her face up to the sun.

He caught her there quite often, the sound of his footsteps drowned out by the sound of water running down the wall and into the pebbles at her feet.

Sometimes he'd bring her a drink, sometimes he'd arrive with the others and they'd have an impromptu barbecue or go down to the beach and play with the children, and sometimes he'd fetch her and take her to the Barrons' house and they'd all play in the pool for hours.

She became great friends with Emily and Georgie, and they gave her lots of helpful advice about babies, as well as some that wasn't helpful at all! And lots of equipment, to go with the things that Dan had insisted they buy. She wasn't sure if the girls knew about the quantum shift in her relationship with Daniel, but she wasn't going to be the one to tell them, and nothing was said, but she had a feeling that Emily, at least, suspected something.

'You're good for him,' she said one day. 'I can't believe the change in such a short time. He's opened up such a lot.'

But she didn't say any more, and nor did Iona. If Dan wanted his sister to know, he'd tell her. Until then, she was quite happy for their private time together to remain just that, and it did.

It was a wonderful, glorious summer, and she felt rested and at peace.

Until she went to the doctor for a check-up, and her blood pressure was high.

'Are you worried about anything?'

Not consciously, she thought, but the future was unknowable and that might be preying on her mind. There was still the business of the will and the DNA test to sort out, but she'd been shutting it out.

'Maybe,' she said. 'But nothing major.'

'You have to rest,' she was told, and so even the pottering came to an end. Daniel spent more time at home, and she spent more time in the garden lying on the bench with her toes trailing in the water, feeling guilty for doing nothing and waiting for her baby to come.

And then she did—two weeks after Daniel had built the cot in her other bedroom—bringing their blissful idyll to an end.

It was four in the morning, and the sun was just edging up over the horizon when she felt the first tightening, low down in her abdomen.

She got quietly out of bed without disturbing him and went downstairs. They'd taken to using his room because he had the phone and the radio alarm clock by the bed, but she still used her room in the day if she lay down for a rest, and she went there now and sat up, propped against the pillows with her legs crossed, and watched the sun come up and waited.

By five she was uncomfortable. By six she was pacing. By seven she was in the car on the way to the hospital, filled with regret that she couldn't have the baby at home but accepting the wisdom of it.

'You OK?' Daniel asked when she sucked her breath in, and she breathed through the contraction and gave him a smile.

'I'm fine,' she said.

Fine?

It was the most terrifying day of his life. He'd never knowingly come within a hundred miles of a labouring woman, and he had absolutely no idea what to do.

'Just hold her and talk to her and remind her to breathe,' Emily told him when he rang in a panic after he'd been sent out so they could examine her. 'Do you want me to come and take over?'

He thought about it—thought about missing the baby's birth, and how he'd feel—and said, 'No. I'll cope. I'll be in touch.'

'You can come back in now, Daniel,' the midwife said, and he took a nice deep breath of hospital air and went back into the labour room.

'She's seven centimetres,' he was told, as if that was meant to mean anything, but the midwife must have seen his blank look and she smiled. 'Ten means she can push.'

'Ah. Right. Thanks.' And he wondered why on earth he hadn't read anything about it or thought about this bit at all. Because he'd been blanking out the baby? Trying not to think about the child put there in her body by another man? A man who, if he weren't already dead, Daniel would have liked to kill with his bare hands for doing all this to her.

He made himself relax then, straightened out his fists, flexed them, reached for her hand and gripped it, and gradually, bit by bit, her body let go and the baby came.

And when she was born, when the squalling, slippery little thing that was her daughter was laid on her bare chest, heart to heart, and he saw Iona's hands curve protectively over the tiny little back and hold her tight, he felt a lump in his throat so big he could hardly swallow it.

'Clever girl,' he said, bending to kiss her cheek, appalled by the blood and the violence of it all and staggered by the fact that his sister had done this—was going to do it again, in fact, apparently—that Georgie had done it, and his own mother, and everybody's mother.

Left up to him, there would only have ever been one child before the whole process got referred back to the designer for a thorough review. He let his breath out on a long sigh, ran his hand round the back of his neck and met her tearful, happy smile with an unsteady one of his own. 'Are you OK?'

She laughed a little shakily. 'I'm fine. Say hello to Lily.'

'Lily?' He smiled. 'Lily. Hello, Lily. It's nice to meet you,' he said, and touched her tiny hand

with his finger. Immediately she gripped it, the
strength of those tiny fingers startling, and he
swallowed hard and stroked them with his thumb,
afraid he'd break her because she was so small.

He was sent out while they cleaned them both
up, and he phoned Emily. 'She's had her. She's
called her Lily,' he said, his voice cracking,
and Emily shrieked in his ear and called to
Harry, and then Harry was on the phone con-
gratulating him.

'Me?' he said, giving a shocked laugh. 'She's
all Iona's work; she's nothing to do with me.'

And even though it was true, it hit him like a
sledgehammer. Lily wasn't anything to do with
him, no matter how magical, how beautiful, how
utterly perfect she was. She was Iona's, and he'd
do well to remember it.

She was amazing.

Tiny, perfect—and everything was like a
dream until Daniel took them home that evening.

To her flat.

He'd changed the sheets, made up the cot and

put the pram in her room with new little sheets and blankets on it.

The midwife came and made sure everything was all right and that she was settled, said she'd see her in the morning and left. And after he'd brought her a hot drink and tucked her up in bed and made sure she was all right, he, too, headed for the door.

'Where are you going?' she asked, wondering if he could hear the note of panic.

He stopped and turned back. 'Next door. I don't want to disturb you. I won't be far away if you need me.'

She wanted to say, I need you now! You won't disturb me, but something in his face stopped her, so she nodded numbly. 'Thanks,' she said instead, and he left the room, pulling the door to.

She stared at it. Not shut, not quite, but almost. Shut enough so he couldn't see her, but not enough that she could cry in peace. And she wanted to cry, because they hadn't slept apart since that first night together, and she missed him!

Well, that was stupid of her, wasn't it? He'd told her he was damaged goods. Clearly he'd meant it, or he would have realised that she needed him beside her more than she needed not to be disturbed.

Which was a joke in itself, because Lily had decided that being awake and able to make noises was great, and that was what she was going to do. All night.

Iona had no idea what to do for her. Was she hungry? She wasn't crying, but if she picked her up, would that wake her so she had to feed her? And she wasn't sure she could get her to latch on without help. She'd struggled in the hospital, but she was adamant that she was going to breast-feed and now she was face to face with the reality of single parenting.

Alone, in the night, with a very new baby and not a single parenting skill to her name.

She swallowed hard and sat up, easing herself carefully back against the pillows. She hurt. Everything hurt, but especially *there*, and she found herself longing for a bath. Could she do it? On her own? Because she could hardly ask Daniel to help her, in the middle of the night.

She ran the water and eased off her nightdress, the same one Georgie had lent her, the one she'd been wearing the night Pebbles had died. The one he'd taken off her that very first time.

He'd thought she was beautiful, but she looked down now at her stomach, hanging like a bag of jelly on her front, and she had to fight back the tears. It was temporary, she told herself. It would soon firm up and go back to normal.

If she could only remember what normal was.

She had one foot in the bath and the other on the floor when Daniel knocked on the door.

'Iona? Are you OK?'

'I'm fine,' she lied, wincing as she lifted the other foot in. Now all she had to do was sit down. Hah. 'I'm in the bath.' Sort of.

'Can I come in?'

She opened her mouth to say no, but he was coming in anyway, his eyes concerned, and tutting under his breath, he came and held her under her arms and lowered her gently into the water. The lovely, lovely, warm water.

It felt fabulous.

Wonderful. Now if only Daniel wasn't standing there looking at her trashed body, she could lie back and enjoy it...

'I'll leave you in peace. Give me a shout when you want to get out and I'll give you a hand.'

He closed the door and she lay back with a sigh of relief. Oh, that was better. So soothing.

She closed her eyes and let herself drift away to a safe place, a quiet, gentle place, tranquil.

She was in the courtyard, her feet on the edge of the water, the sound soothing her and blanking out all the chaos in the world. Brian was there with her, watching her, a smile on his face, and Jamie was behind him. He looked at her—no, through her—and turned and walked away.

She let him go. She had no way of holding him, and she didn't want to. He needed to be free, and so did she. Wonderfully, marvellously free.

She opened her eyes, to find Daniel sitting there on a chair, watching her. 'Oh,' she said, surprised and yet not. She had felt someone was watching over her. She'd thought it was Brian, but maybe it had been Daniel she'd sensed. And where had the chair come from? She stifled the ridiculous urge to cover her body with her hands. He'd been watching her for however long, and sayings about stable doors and bolting horses came to mind.

'How long have you been there?'

'Ten minutes? You've been in there ages. You fell asleep, and I didn't want to leave you. The water must be cold now—do you want a hand out?'

'I need to wash, first,' she said, and expected him to leave, but he didn't. He ran more hot water into the bath, took a new flannel from the shelf and soaped it thoroughly, then, sitting her up, he washed her back, his hands gentle and yet thorough. He slid down her arms, under them, over her breasts, down her legs—even between her toes. And then he rinsed her just as carefully, and helped her out.

His hands were strong and sure, and the moment she was on her feet, there was a warm towel to wrap her in, and he helped her over to the chair. 'Give me a call if you need me,' he said, and tactfully left her alone to do the things she needed to do after giving birth.

She slipped her nightdress on and went back into the bedroom, to find him standing there with Lily in his arms.

'She was crying,' he said softly, but she wasn't crying now. She was lying staring up at him, her eyes wide open, locked on his, and she felt a huge lump in her throat. He looked so comfortable with her, so natural. Of course he'd had Kizzy and Lucie to practise on, and with all the blatant fecundity of his close circle of family and friends he was no stranger to children.

What a terrible shame that he wouldn't be there for Lily, too. Because he wouldn't. She knew that. She was just his housekeeper, and he was way out of her league. He might be kindness itself, and he might have diverted himself with her, but that was all. And the moment the DNA test had been done and her claim for Lily had been proved, she'd be out. The only light at the end of the tunnel was that there had been no sign of the will. They'd torn the place apart now, and there was nowhere else it could be, really. Her last chance, Brian's office, had proved a barren hope when they'd moved their site office out into a Portakabin and gutted the room.

Nothing. Not under the floorboards, or tucked under the carpet—nowhere.

And without it, there was a chance she'd get nothing.

Foolish woman that she was, she was almost clinging now to the hope that it didn't turn up, that she did get nothing, because, given enough time, maybe Daniel would realise that he loved her as much as she loved him.

She felt her legs go weak, and sat down abruptly on the edge of the bed. She loved him?

Well, of course she loved him. She knew it. It was just that the words had popped into her mind and shocked her. They were just so—so *significant*.

'I think she's hungry,' he said, bringing the baby over to her, and she settled herself back against the pillows, pulled up the quilt and took the baby from him.

'I can manage now,' she lied, clinging to the

remnants of her pride, and he nodded abruptly and walked out, pulling the door to again.

She opened the front of the nightdress, pushed it aside and turned Lily towards her. Now. Brush her nipple against the baby's cheek—so. Then as she turns, push her head—done it! The crying stopped, replaced by a surprisingly loud, rhythmic sucking noise that nearly made her laugh out loud.

And she stopped worrying about the will, stopped thinking about Daniel, and settled down, comfortable at last, to enjoy her beautiful little girl.

The next few days were a time of adjustment, but to his untutored eye, at least, Iona seemed to be taking to motherhood like a duck to water.

Daniel made sure he was never far away, and if she missed him at night, she didn't say so.

After that first night, she never once asked for his help. After a week, when she was clearly all right without him, he moved back up to his own bedroom with a strange sense of regret. If he'd just slept with her the night he'd brought her home—held her in his arms, or lain beside her holding hands—maybe they would have still been close, but there was something distant about their new relationship, something remote, that saddened him, because he knew their little interlude was over.

She was a mother now, and the time for dreams was over. She settled into a sort of routine with Lily, and Emily and Georgie were amazed at what a good, easy baby she was.

She had so many cuddles it was a wonder she knew who her mother was, he thought, and because he didn't want Iona to feel that she had to do anything except spend time with Lily, he was trying to keep the place clean and tidy.

'You need a housekeeper,' Harry teased one day when he'd dropped in with Emily and the kids on their way back from the beach. He just shot him a look and carried on scrubbing the sink.

'It's only for a little while, but if I don't do it or get someone in, she'll feel she has to, just because she's like that.'

Harry propped himself up against the wall and

studied him thoughtfully. 'So how long are you going to go on kidding yourself that she's just a housekeeper?'

Dan threw the scourer back into the sink and straightened up, staring down the garden to where the girls were sitting on the grass with all the children. She was feeding Lily, and his heart contracted. 'Well, what the hell else is she?' he growled.

Harry shrugged, following his gaze down the garden to the happy little group. 'I don't know. Your girlfriend? Your companion? The woman you love?'

He swallowed hard and turned back to the sink. 'I don't love her,' he said. 'I don't do relationships.'

'Well, it looks to me like you do relationships. You just don't know what to call them.'

'Hazardous,' he growled. 'Complicated. Unnecessary.'

'Oh, I'm with you on the first two, but unnecessary? No way.' Harry's voice lowered. 'You need her, Daniel. And she needs you. Don't close your mind.'

'This from the man who was telling me not to get involved?' he said incredulously, and Harry gave a wry laugh.

'Yeah, well, that was before I met her.'

'So what's changed?'

'You have,' Harry said quietly. 'You're happy. Contented. You've let it all go—all the Kate stuff.'

'What Kate stuff?' God, he'd kill Iona if she'd told him—

'Whatever happened. I have no idea. I guess she cheated on you. God knows why; she wouldn't find a better man.'

He gave a soft snort and rinsed out the cloth he'd been using to wipe down the cupboards. Funny, when Iona did them, they had a wonderful streak-free shine. Now, they looked as if a two-year-old had been let loose with a grubby rag. They'd been better before—

'OK, don't talk about it,' Harry said with a sigh. 'But think about it. Think about Iona, and what she means to you. And don't let her slip through your fingers, Dan. She's a darling.

Clever, funny, intelligent, well-read, provoca-
tive, generous to a fault—'

'Leave her alone,' Dan snarled, turning on him
with a glare. 'You're married. Don't forget that.
And if you mess my sister about, I'll kill you.'

Harry held his hands up in surrender. 'I have no
intention of messing your sister about. I love her
to bits. That doesn't make me blind and insensi-
tive, though, and if you've got any sense, you'll
open your own eyes and pay a bit of heed to
what's right under your nose. Iona's the best thing
that's ever happened to you. Don't let her go.'

And, without another word, he walked out of
the door and down the garden to join the others.

Daniel snapped his jaw shut and turned back
to the cupboards. God, they were awful. He got
the cloth out and tried again.

CHAPTER TEN

THE days turned to weeks, and Dan couldn't justify hanging around for Iona any more. She was well, she was fit, and anyway she had Emily and Georgie if she needed any help or advice.

Both of them were much better equipped in that department than he was, so with a strange feeling of redundancy, he went back to work at the hotel.

And not before time.

He'd really taken his eye off the ball, he thought, when he walked into the foyer and found the old reception desk—the central feature of the foyer, the desk that Iona loved so much— had been ripped out to leave a yawning void.

He found George in the area where the annexe had been, supervising the setting out. 'Where's the desk?' he asked, trying to keep a lid on his boiling emotions.

George frowned. 'It's outside. The boys only took it out this morning, but you said you wanted the fittings all cleared and it was the last thing.' He tipped his head on one side. 'I did wonder if you meant the desk, but the boys had done it before I realised. It's still in one piece. It's a lovely thing, actually. Very heavy. It's solid mahogany. Seems a shame to chuck it out. The shelves are there, too. We thought you might have plans for them.'

He felt his shoulders drop a little. 'I do. We're going to get it restored. It needed to come out, but carefully.'

George looked insulted. 'They took it out carefully, Dan. Go and have a look at it—it's just by the site office.'

So he went and stood behind it, where generations of staff would have stood to welcome their guests, placing his hands flat down on to it. The top was battered, scarred by the passage of many keys, the old wood gleaming even through the dust, and he ran his hand over it, feeling its history with his fingertips. He'd seen Iona doing that, touching it lovingly. That was why he wanted to keep it, he realised. Not because the hotel needed it. In fact working it into the scheme would be a bit of a nightmare.

But Iona loved it, and that was good enough for him.

He dropped down on to his haunches, peering up underneath the inside, into the recess formed by a shelf that was set about nine inches down from the top, to see if he could work out how the top was fixed. Maybe they should just keep that bit...

He couldn't really see. The September sun was so bright it threw the recess into deep shadow, but there was something stuck on it. Something white—a long rectangle taped to the underside. He reached up, feeling it with his fingers. An envelope?

Peeling it away, he stood up, the envelope in his hands, and stared at it.

'Copy of The Last Will of Brian Henry Dawes', it said on the outside, and the date was the tenth of March. Six months ago, and just a few weeks before Brian had died.

And the original will, it stated, was lodged with Cooper, Farringdon, Solicitors, 29 High Street, Yoxburgh. Not Barry Edwards. Which was why he'd had no knowledge of it.

Dan was standing there with it in his hands when Nick pulled into the car park and came over to him. 'What's that?' he asked, and Daniel held it out to him.

He took it, read the outside and blinked. 'Right,' he said slowly. 'Where did you find it?'

'Sellotaped under the desk,' he said.

'Well, why on earth would he put it there? And why use a solicitor who wasn't his usual one?'

'Because he didn't trust Ian? Because he knew it would be found when the hotel was refurbished? Or because he wasn't sure about it?' Dan didn't know, but he knew one thing. He had to tell Iona, and they had to open it and read the contents.

'I think we need to contact our solicitor,' Nick said, reading his mind. 'Leave it with me. I'll take it there, we'll get him to see us now. You go and get Iona—tell her to leave the baby with Georgie, if she doesn't want to bring her.'

Dan drove home, the tension making his muscles tight and his heart pound. What did the will contain? And what would the significance be for Iona and Lily?

And for him?

'You're home early.'

He looked worried—no, not worried. Cautious. As if he had bad news. She'd seen enough of those looks recently to last a lifetime, and she sat back down on the bench in the courtyard and stared at him, her heart starting to pound.

'Daniel, what is it?'

He frowned slightly. 'We've found the will.'

Her hand flew to her chest, holding down the surge of emotion that rushed through it, and she closed her eyes and counted to ten.

'Have you got it?' she asked, her voice rusty with shock.

'Nick's got it. He's taken it to the solicitor. We thought it should be opened officially.'

'Oh. Right. Yes—yes, of course. So—will he tell us what's in it?'

'I don't know. It's only a copy. He needs to contact the solicitor who's got the original.'

'Barry Edwards?'

He shook his head. 'No. Not Edwards. It's apparently with Cooper, Farringdon.'

Light dawned. 'Mike Cooper—of course! He was there a few times a couple of months before Brian died, but then I didn't see him again. He retired a while ago. He used to come in and see him from time to time. He was a friend, I think. We used to put up clients for him on occasions, but I thought by the time Brian died, he'd been retired for ages.' She shook her head to try and clear it. 'So—where did you find it?'

'Under the reception desk, taped under the top.'

She closed her eyes, wondering how she could have been so stupid. 'On the right?'

'Yes. Why?'

She laughed, because it was so obvious. 'He said something to me in the hospital, just before he died. He told me he'd taken care of me, and said "Check it out". He said it two or three times, but he was so unwell I didn't want to press him, so I told him not to worry. I didn't understand the significance at the time, but when people were checking out, that was where we put the paperwork—on the right-hand side of the desk, on the shelf underneath. Hence "check it out". Oh, I can't believe I didn't think of it!'

She stood up, her legs trembling. 'Can we go and talk to him? To Mike Cooper?'

'I think our solicitor's setting it up.'

'Good.'

Then she would know, one way or the other, what her options were. She was very much afraid they didn't include Daniel.

Since she'd had the baby, although he'd been kindness itself, he hadn't been near her. He hadn't held her, hadn't touched her, hadn't kissed her—OK, her body wasn't ready for more than that yet, but it didn't have to be all or nothing, did it? And if he was keeping such a distance from her, it could only mean that he'd been looking for a diversion and she'd been available—and now she wasn't, he didn't want to know. Oh, well, she'd told him she wasn't asking for eternity, and he'd obviously taken her at her word.

The knowledge was bitter, and the will that only a few weeks ago she had been dreading, now seemed like her way out of an impossible and painful situation.

Not that she expected much. A few thousand, hopefully? Enough to put down a deposit on a little house, so she could work and pay a small mortgage and give Lily some kind of lifestyle. That was all she wanted. Just enough of a leg-up to give her some security. Then she could stop worrying about the future and get on with their lives.

They couldn't see Mike Cooper until late that afternoon, to give Ian Dawes time to come from London. The fact that he was prepared to come in such a hurry was interesting, as was his face when he saw Iona there in Mike's old chambers with the baby.

'It's born,' he said blankly, as if he hadn't

expected there to be a child. Or had hoped there wouldn't be? Well, tough, Daniel thought, and hoped Iona would be up to dealing with his hostility. Apparently so.

'It's September, Ian,' she said, and Dan wouldn't have been surprised if she'd rolled her eyes. 'I got pregnant when Jamie was home in November. I'm not an elephant. Lily, say hello to Uncle Ian,' she added pointedly.

The man frowned, and Daniel wanted to kill him. He still obviously didn't believe that Lily was his brother's child, but the DNA test was under way—at least Lily's part of it. Ian had refused to co-operate until there was a need proved by a valid will or a court of law. Dragging it out to the bitter end.

And now there they were, in Mike Cooper's old office, and Cooper was straightening out the document and smiling at Iona. 'So this is the baby? Well, hello, little one. Goodness, she's the spitting image of her father,' he said with a smile, and then resumed his seat, steepled his fingers over the will on his desk and ran his eyes over them all.

'First, let me apologise for the delay in reveal-

ing the contents of the will to you. Because I'c
retired, I was unaware of my client's death until
I received a call from my office earlier today, anc
he obviously hadn't made the whereabouts of the
will known to you all. Still, we're here now, so if
we're all ready?' he said, and then started to read.

It was gobbledegook. Well, to most people it
would be. To Iona, who'd studied law, it was just
legal jargon.

But it was legal, signed and witnessed, and as
Brian had promised, he'd taken care of Lily.

Mike Cooper read:

'To my son Ian I leave the sum of ten thousand pounds. Of the balance of the residuary
estate, the Trustees shall hold one half in trust
equally for such surviving child or children
of my late son James, whether born or *en
ventre sa mère*. Subject to that—'

She didn't hear the rest, because Ian was
making such a noise he was drowning Mike out.

He took off his glasses, looked up at Ian and said, 'Mr Dawes, I would appreciate it if we could conduct this in a proper and formal manner, without interruption.' Then he carried on reading, but she'd tuned him out, staring down at her baby in a state of shock.

She swallowed. Half? He'd really left Lily half? And Ian only ten thousand pounds? Not that she knew how much half was, but surely that couldn't be right? It must be more than ten thousand, unless Brian's debts had been absolutely enormous. Which was quite possible—

On the other side of the room Ian was fulminating, but all she could do was stare down at Lily in her arms and shake her head in disbelief.

He'd done it. Dear, darling Brian, who'd never got round to anything, had found time, even when he'd been so ill, to ensure Lily's future.

'Will there be enough to put down a deposit to buy her a little house?' she said, and Mike Cooper chuckled.

'I should think so, my dear. The hotel sold for in excess of one and three-quarter million pounds. Once the debts are cleared and the inheritance tax paid, I understand from Barry Edwards that there will be a little over a million pounds, of which half will belong to Lily, and you and I have that in trust for her, for you to use as we see fit, until she reaches the age of eighteen. The other half, of course, is yours to do with as you wish. So, yes, you can buy a house. A very nice house.'

Now he really was talking gobbledegook. She stared at him. 'Mine?' she said, puzzled. 'Why mine?'

'Because those are the terms of the will.' He read it again, and this time she heard it.

'—one half of my residuary estate I leave to Iona Lockwood, for her care and compassion and unfailing consideration of me; in the event that there is no surviving child of my son James, then the whole balance of the residual estate to go to Iona Lockwood.

'He's left ten thousand pounds to his son, and of the rest, half to Lily, in trust, and half to you, my dear. And if anything should happen to Lily, then you inherit her half.'

'Me?' She turned and stared at Daniel, who was looking as stunned as she felt.

'Only if she's James's daughter,' Ian said, finally finding his voice again. 'And that's yet to be proved. If she's not James's daughter, then it should come to me! Dammit, it should all come to me! What the hell was the stupid old bastard thinking about—'

'Mr Dawes!' Mike Cooper roared, lumbering to his feet and making Lily stiffen with shock. 'I will not have this language in my chambers! During the course of the preparation of this will, I had lengthy discourse with your father, and through it all he had nothing but praise for Miss Lockwood and concern for her future. She asked for nothing, she worked for no salary, and she was tireless in her care of him. All he ever said of you was that you had been a selfish, vindictive little boy and you'd turned into a selfish, vindictive little man. And there is no provision for the money to come to you. The wording is precise. No sur-

viving child. If this child is not that of your brother
James, then there is no surviving child, in which
case the whole would go to Miss Lockwood
anyway. All you are entitled to is the ten thousand
pounds stipulated by the will.'

'I'll contest it!'

'You are, of course, at liberty to do so, but I
have to tell you that your father was in sound
mind when this will was made, and it was
written with great consideration and after much
thought. Your chances of winning are so slight I
would say they do not exist, but if that is how
you wish to spend your legacy, it's your prero-
gative, but I haven't come out of my retirement
to listen to any more of your nonsense.'

He turned to Iona, who was still sitting there
in stunned silence, staring at him and shushing
Lily on autopilot. 'Miss Lockwood, I have here
a copy of the will for you to study. I'm sure,
being a law student, you'll understand its ramifi-
cations, but if you require any clarification, give
me a call. I'd be delighted to explain it to you.
Mr Dawes? Your copy,' he said, handing it over

without volunteering any explanation, and Iona had to bite her lip.

Ian was furious, and getting crosser by the minute, and she had to remind herself not to feel sorry for him.

'You'll be hearing from my lawyers!' he yelled, leaving the room and slamming the door behind him.

Or attempting to. It was on a closer, though, and all he did was hurt his hand. He swore, threw them all a furious glare and strode off down the corridor.

'Oops,' she said softly, and Mike Cooper smiled.

'Indeed,' he said. 'Now, is there anything else I can help you with, or can I get back to my golf?'

'I can't keep it.'

They were sitting on the steps at the end of the garden, staring out over the moonlit sea, and Iona was mulling over the afternoon's events and toying idly with a glass of champagne.

Just the one, because of feeding Lily, but they were supposedly celebrating. Daniel, not being restricted by motherhood, poured himself another one and set the bottle down on the step beside them.

'Why can't you keep it?'

'Because I ought to give it to Ian.'

'Ian?' He nearly choked on the champagne. 'Iona, are you nuts? He's a nasty piece of work. Even his own father recognised that. That's why he gave him such a token pay-off.'

'No,' she said, shaking her head. 'I've worked it out. He gave him ten thousand because that's what he'd given Jamie over the previous few months before his death, and he was nothing if not fair and even-handed. But I just feel guilty— as if everyone's looking at me and thinking I wormed my way into his affections and conned him into changing his will—'

'Rubbish. You were wonderful to him when neither of his sons could be bothered to lift a finger. Nick said the place wouldn't have been running without you. You know he said he thought of you as a daughter?'

She stared at him. 'Really?'

'Really. That was how he described you to

Mike Cooper, apparently. He genuinely loved you, Iona.'

'Gosh.' She swallowed the sudden lump in her throat and stared down at her hands. 'He was wonderful to me. I really miss him.'

'Well, you'll be able to think of him every time you walk up to your front door and put the key in it and let yourself into your very own home. That's a fitting legacy, don't you think?'

Oh, God, how lonely. Even if she'd have Lily for company. *I don't want to do that! I don't want my own front door! I want yours—I want you to ask me to stay here with you, to tell me you love me. Not tell me that moving out into a house of my own would be a fitting legacy, for heaven's sake!*

'Yes, it would, wouldn't it?' she said, throwing him a probably very unconvincing smile. 'If I keep it.'

'Well, you'll have to keep Lily's half, you don't have a choice, and as a long-term investment, property has out-performed all other forms of investment substantially over the past thirty-odd years, so buying a house with it would be the only sensible thing to do. And, as for your half, what would you do with it? Apart from give it to Ian. I might have to kill you to stop you doing that,' he said mildly. 'The man's a waste of a good skin.'

The bit of her that wasn't screaming inside about out-performing investments actually managed a laugh. 'So what else would I do with it?' She shrugged. 'Give it to charity? Nick does a lot for charity, Georgie says. I could ask him.'

'You could finish your degree,' he suggested, more seriously now. 'Get qualified, and set up a foundation to help with legal fees for people who can't afford to fight for their rights. You wanted to be a human rights lawyer—here's your chance. You could call it the Brian Dawes Foundation in his memory.'

What a wonderful idea. 'I could,' she said slowly. 'That would be a better use of it. He'd approve of that. Thank you.'

She rubbed her temples. She had a headache,

probably brought on by the stress of the afternoon and Ian's vitriolic outburst. She stood up and brushed off her skirt, and it billowed round her ankles in the light sea breeze. 'Daniel, do you mind if I have an early night? I'm feeling a bit shell-shocked.' *And I need to go and cry my eyes out, because all you seem to be able to talk about is me going, and I don't think I can bear it...*

'Sure.' He stood up and walked back in with her. 'Can I get you anything?'

She shook her head. 'No, I'm fine. Thank you for coming with me today.'

'You're welcome.'

She hesitated, gave him a chance to hug her, to kiss her goodnight—dammit, anything at all—but he just stood there and waited, so she turned on her heel and walked down the hall into her flat, closed the door and started to cry.

'So what the hell is this about Iona moving? I thought she was going to buy some kind of investment property?' Emily asked, plonking herself down on his sofa and rubbing her hands over her gently expanding middle while she interrogated him.

He looked startled. 'No. Of course not. Well, only incidentally. She's going to buy a house and move into it. What's so odd about that? It's the obvious thing to do, I should have thought.'

'Really?' Emily looked stunned. 'But what about you two?'

'What about us two? What us two? And anyway, there are three—'

She growled and rolled her eyes. 'God, you're so obtuse. For heaven's sake, Dan, I thought you loved each other.'

He blinked. 'What the hell gave you that idea?'

'Oh, dear. I've seen you together?' she said, as if he was a slightly dense toddler.

When? Because certainly since she'd had the baby he'd kept himself as far away from her as he could without actively ostracising her. 'You're imagining it,' he said flatly.

'Am I? I don't think so. You're really close. Or you were before she had the baby. Lots of lingering glances and little touches—it was obvious. A blind man on a galloping horse could see you were in love.' She frowned. 'Although since then you've been a little distant—'

'She doesn't love me, don't be ridiculous—and anyway she's had a baby!'

'Well, it's not exactly some foul disease, Dan! And why is it ridiculous? Just because she's had someone else's baby doesn't stop her loving you, and it shouldn't stop you being nice to her. You can still cuddle her. And you haven't,' she said accusingly. 'I thought she was looking a bit glum. I thought it was the will thing, but when I spoke to her earlier on the phone, she didn't sound too happy, and I've been thinking about it.'

'Oh, God help us,' Dan said, rolling his eyes, and she gave a tiny little scream of frustration.

'Dan, I'm serious,' she said. 'She loves you to bits. And you love her. You do love her,' she said again, when he opened his mouth to argue. 'You know you do. So when are you going to admit it?'

He swallowed hard and rested his head back on the sofa, closing his eyes. 'She doesn't love me, Em,' he said gruffly. 'She's still in love with Jamie.'

'Oh, rubbish! She's no such thing! She outgrew him years ago, Dan—he was little better than his brother. Nicer, but just as idle and unhelpful. She loves you, Daniel, and she needs a real man— one who's grown-up enough to love her back. A man like you—kind and thoughtful and safe.'

'Oh, God, damned by faint praise,' he said, and Emily rolled her eyes and dropped back against the sofa.

'Is that what you think? Faint praise? Look at her life, Dan! Those are the most important things you could give her. That and your love. So when are you going to tell her you love her? When are you going to tell her you don't want her to move out, you want her to stay here and marry you and spend her life with you, so you can be part of Lily's life and watch her grow up and give her brothers and sisters—?'

'Enough! For God's sake, Em, that's enough!' he said, panicking, his palms breaking out in a cold sweat. 'I can't do that.'

'Why?' she asked, relentless. 'Because Kate cheated on you? Iona isn't Kate. Kate was a real piece of work. She never loved you, but Iona does; she loves you with all her heart, and she'll never cheat on you or lie to you or hurt you, and she needs to know you love her back.'

He sat forward. 'You really think that? That she loves me?' He shook his head. 'She's still grieving—'

'No! No, Dan, no, no, no! She's over him! It's you she loves. You have to tell her.'

He swallowed, remembering Kate, when he'd found out about her and Angie, when he'd said he loved her, thought she'd loved him, and she'd just laughed at him. Thrown back her head and laughed—

'What if I tell her all that and she laughs at me?' he said, his voice uneven.

Emily frowned. 'She won't. But what if she did? So what? What have you lost? Just pride. What's that, compared to a lifetime of loving her?' She sat down beside him, sliding her arms round him and hugging him. 'Give her a chance, Dan,' she pleaded. 'Give both of you a chance. Go and talk to her now.'

He shook his head. 'She's asleep. She wanted an early night.'

'So why's she standing at the end of the garden looking at the sea as if she'd like to throw herself in it?'

She stood up, kissed his cheek and left him sitting there staring out of the window at Iona.

The woman he loved. The only woman he'd ever really loved, he realised. Please, God, she wouldn't laugh at him.

He got to his feet and walked slowly, mechanically, to the door and slid it open, going out into the night. It had been a warm day, but now there was a chill in the air—or was it fear making him cold?

He swallowed, took a deep breath and started walking down the lawn.

She didn't hear him coming, but she felt his presence and turned as he reached her.

'Hi, there,' he said, and she scanned his face. He looked grave, and she gave him an unsteady smile in the moonlight. Was this it? The grand goodbye?

'Hi,' she managed.

'I thought you were having an early night?'

'I couldn't sleep. I just needed to hear the sea.'

'Want me to leave you alone?'

She shook her head, wondering if he could see the tears on her cheeks or if they'd dried in the wind. 'Not really. I was just thinking about Brian.'

He sat down on the top step and patted the stone beside him. After a long pause, she sat down, and he took her hand and rubbed it softly, his thumb grazing over the back of it, slowly, back and forth. 'You really miss him, don't you?' he murmured. 'You've had a tough year.'

She nodded, thinking back over it. Tough? It had been momentous. 'What with watching Brian fall apart over Jamie's death, and then seeing him die just when he was about to retire and put his feet up and have the rest he so badly deserved—' She shook her head, remembering his awful, bitter disappointment in his sons, the shocking deterioration of his health, his death. 'If only Jamie had helped, or Ian, but they were as bad as each other. Neither of them cared about him, and he was such a good man. He deserved better from his sons.'

His thumb stilled, and he turned his head and looked at her. 'I thought you loved Jamie?' he asked quietly, and she shrugged.

'Did I? I don't know. Maybe once, or maybe he was just fun and I was bored of travelling alone and it was good to have company. If I'm honest, I think I was just lonely, and if I hadn't met him I would have gone back to Maastricht as I'd planned. But then I came here and met Brian, and he made me so welcome, and for the first time in my life I had a proper base. Somewhere I could call home—even if it was a shabby old hotel with a derelict annexe and an even more derelict cat—'

She gave an unsteady laugh and looked towards the lilac. 'He was the only father I've ever known, and he gave me my first real home, my first pet. Poor little Pebbles. Still, at least she got to die here, under a bush in the sun, without pain. I can't think of a more beautiful place to die.'

'Or live?' he said tentatively, and she looked

at him, hardly daring to hope. 'Is it a beautiful place to live?'

'Here?' She turned and stared at the house, wondering what he meant. Not that, surely. He was talking about the out-performing damned investments again. She sighed. 'It's a beautiful place to live, but I could never afford something like this, and anyway, I couldn't justify it. I can't possibly keep all that money and spend it, Dan. I'm not like that. I find it really hard to cope with Nick and Georgie having so much money, and the fact that you're a millionaire and Harry's got such huge advances for his memoirs, and everything's such big numbers, you know? When I met you, I said I had to go out and find some food. I didn't mean it literally, not quite, but Ian had given me five hundred pounds at the funeral, and I was going to have to make it last, but with the power off, I could only eat things that didn't need cooking—so no cheap pasta. I can't tell you how sick I was of cold baked beans and tuna sandwiches. That Chinese take-away was the first hot food I'd had in six weeks.'

He looked shocked. Shocked and horrified, and she wanted to slide her arms round him and tell him it was all right, she'd survived, but he was looking at her oddly, as if he didn't quite know what to say, and she turned away, looking back out over the sea and wishing she could just tell him how she felt…

'Marry me,' he blurted out, and she turned and stared at him in astonishment.

'What?'

'I said marry me,' he repeated, but this time in a calmer, surer voice, as if having said it out loud, it suddenly seemed like the most sensible thing in the world. 'Marry me and let me love you. Because I do love you, you know. I've loved you since I caught you dragging that mattress out of the skip, and I know I've been a bit slow on the uptake, but I really thought you were still in love with Jamie, and it was Emily who told me not to be so dense.'

Emily? Bless her heart. She was a good friend.

She thought back to the time after the baby's birth, to her loneliness and isolation when he'd been so remote. 'Really? You love me? Then why've you been keeping me at arm's length since I had the baby, Daniel? Why didn't you stay with me? Why didn't you *tell* me?'

He shrugged, as if he was looking inside himself and finding the awkward truth. 'I think—I felt that Lily was Jamie's, and it was as if you were with him then, because you were with her, and she's a part of him. And I felt as if I didn't belong, as if I was intruding on something private.'

She started to smile, a slow smile that lit up the depths of her eyes as she stared up into his beautiful, beloved face.

'Oh, Daniel,' she said softly, reaching up and touching her fingers gently to his cheek. 'Of course you belonged. You were there for me when I was at my lowest ebb, and at my highest high. You've been my rock, the only thing that's got me through. You've rescued me from falling ceilings, buried my cat, washed me when I had Lily, changed her nappies, cooked and cleaned and done the laundry so I didn't feel guilty—'

'Did you feel guilty? I didn't want you to feel guilty.'

'Well, I did, but only because I felt it was my job. If I'd thought you were doing it for love, I would have treasured every gesture.' She reached up and pressed a tender, loving kiss to his lips. 'Ask me again, Dan. Ask me to marry you. Ask me to live here with you.'

He swallowed hard, then, taking her hand, he stood up, walked down a few steps and went down on one knee just below her, stared up into her eyes and said, his voice gruff and sincere and steady as a rock, 'I love you, Iona. And I love Lily. Stay with me. Marry me, and live here with me, and turn this ridiculous great house into a home. Help me fill it with children—fostered or adopted, preferably, so I don't have to watch you going through that awful thing all over again, but somehow, some way, help me turn us into a family. A proper family. For ever.'

'Oh, Daniel.'

As she reached for him and lifted her face to his, she could feel the tears tracking down her cheeks—

tears of joy, of happiness, and a love so profound she thought her heart would burst from it.

'Of course I'll marry you,' she said softly. 'I'd marry you and live with you and give you children wherever we lived. This house is just that—a house, but it's a beautiful house, a wonderful house, and I can't think of a better place to make our home. And we'll fill it with children. As many as you want. So long as I'm with you, I couldn't ask for anything more. But I do want to finish my degree, and I want to set up that foundation in memory of Brian, and when Lily's old enough, I'll tell her about her grandfather. Maybe she'll even get to meet her grandmother, if I can ever persuade her to come back to England. She'll love you, by the way.'

'Tough. I'm taken,' he said, wrapping his arms round her and drawing her closer. 'Maybe you could buy a house for Lily as an investment for her, and your mother could live in it?'

'A base?' She laughed. 'Not her thing. I told you, she's a hippy.'

'Even hippies grow old.'

She tipped her head back and looked at him. 'You try to fix everything for everybody, don't you?' she murmured, and kissed him. 'I love you, Daniel Hamilton. You're such a good man. Brian would have liked you, and Mrs Jessop thinks you're wonderful. She'll be really pleased to hear we're getting married. We'll have to invite her to the wedding. She won't be at all surprised.'

He thought of Mrs Jessop, and the knowing look in her wise old eyes as she'd said, 'You'll get there.'

And he smiled down at Iona and feathered a gentle kiss over her lips. 'You know, I don't think she will.'

He kissed her again, and then again, and then in the distance they heard the baby cry.

He lifted his head and gave her a wry smile. 'This may have to wait,' he murmured ruefully, and she smiled back.

'There's no hurry. We've got the rest of our lives,' she said.

And, arm in arm, they walked back up the garden to their home, and their daughter, and their future...

MILLS & BOON PUBLISH EIGHT LARGE PRINT TITLES A MONTH. THESE ARE THE EIGHT TITLES FOR SEPTEMBER 2008.

———— ∅ ————

THE MARKONOS BRIDE
Michelle Reid

THE ITALIAN'S PASSIONATE REVENGE
Lucy Gordon

THE GREEK TYCOON'S BABY BARGAIN
Sharon Kendrick

DI CESARE'S PREGNANT MISTRESS
Chantelle Shaw

HIS PREGNANT HOUSEKEEPER
Caroline Anderson

THE ITALIAN PLAYBOY'S SECRET SON
Rebecca Winters

HER SHEIKH BOSS
Carol Grace

WANTED: WHITE WEDDING
Natasha Oakley

MILLS & BOON®
Pure reading pleasure™

0808 Rom L

MILLS & BOON PUBLISH EIGHT LARGE PRINT TITLES A MONTH. THESE ARE THE EIGHT TITLES FOR OCTOBER 2008.

———————— ✿ ————————

THE SHEIKH'S BLACKMAILED MISTRESS
Penny Jordan

THE MILLIONAIRE'S INEXPERIENCED
LOVE-SLAVE
Miranda Lee

BOUGHT: THE GREEK'S INNOCENT VIRGIN
Sarah Morgan

BEDDED AT THE BILLIONAIRE'S
CONVENIENCE
Cathy Williams

THE PREGNANCY PROMISE
Barbara McMahon

THE ITALIAN'S CINDERELLA BRIDE
Lucy Gordon

SAYING YES TO THE MILLIONAIRE
Fiona Harper

HER ROYAL WEDDING WISH
Cara Colter

MILLS & BOON®
Pure reading pleasure™

0908 R